Stingray

TITLES IN THE LIBRARY OF KOREAN LITERATURE
AVAILABLE FROM DALKEY ARCHIVE PRESS

LIBRARY OF KOREAN LITERATURE
1

Stingray

Kim Joo-young

Translated by

Inrae You Vinciguerra

and

Louis Vinciguerra

DALKEY ARCHIVE PRESS
CHAMPAIGN / LONDON / DUBLIN

Originally published in Korean as *Hongŏ* by Munidang, Seoul, 1998

Copyright © 1998 by Kim Joo-young
Translation © 2013 by Inrae You Vinciguerra and Louis Vinciguerra

First edition, 2013
All rights reserved

Library of Congress Cataloging-in-Publication Data

Kim, Chu-yong, 1939-
[Hongo. English]
Stingray / Kim Joo-young ; translated by Inrae You Vinciguerra and Louis Vinciguerra.
-- First edition.
pages cm
ISBN 978-1-56478-959-4 (acid-free paper)
1. Families--Korea--Fiction. 2. Domestic fiction. I. You, Inrae, translator. II. Vinciguerra, Louis, translator. III. Title.
PL992.415.C529H6613 2013
895.7'14--dc23
2013027140

Partially funded by a grant from the Illinois Arts Council, a state agency

Library of Korean Literature
Published in collaboration with the Literature Translation Institute of Korea

www.dalkeyarchive.com

Cover: design and composition by Mikhail Iliatov

Printed on permanent/durable acid-free paper

1

It was early morning. Snowflakes, white as goose feathers, danced in the air before piling up everywhere.

Although daybreak was approaching, it was still warm in the room. That's why I always slept late on snowy mornings. I could barely hear my mother breathing from the other side of the bed I shared with her. It was as if the falling snow had muffled the sound of her breath.

The room was as quiet as the bottom of a deep sea. And this tranquility, where even time had seemingly stopped, was seducing me into an early morning's sweet sleep.

The sun had risen long before, but the room was still dim. This was because of the snow's magic, something that also gave the villagers an excuse to sleep to their hearts' content.

Right then, I noticed Mother quietly rising and gently slipping away from our bed. She looked very neat and tidy in her nightgown. After she left, I drew the comforter all the way up to my forehead. I heard her saying to herself, "What an incredible amount of snow fell last night . . . it covered up the whole porch." Since she was talking to herself, I didn't reply, but I knew that I had just a little time left to enjoy being lazy in bed. Mother, though, kept talking.

"With you snoring, it was hard to sleep last night."

While she was changing her clothes before going to the kitchen, the room became brighter. I could see her fragile shoulders and fair skin through her thin nightgown.

"Give me a hand here," she said, standing at the front door.

Her voice was tinged with annoyance as she tried to force the door open. Holding the doorknob with both hands, she tried again to push the door open, but with a thick layer of snow on the porch blocking the door, it didn't look like it would be an easy task.

Reluctantly, I got up, and this time both of us tried to force the door open, but regardless of all our effort, we still couldn't open it wide enough for us to move through. And when we finally succeeded in opening it halfway, a white world unfolded outside—we were dumbstruck. I had never seen so much snow in my whole life! Mother reached for my hand and held it tightly.

Enchanted by the swirling snow, we sat on the floor, motionless, watching the snow-white world. Gently, Mother held her *jeo-go-ri* against her bosom.

"I've never seen this much snow . . . it's amazing," she said, softly.

Halfway down the paper door, the snow had already dampened the paper. Mother put on a warm, quilted *jeo-go-ri* padded with cotton. It was then that I heard someone snoring somewhere.

"Mother, do you hear the snoring?" I asked.

At that moment the sound suddenly stopped. The room was now silent.

"Maybe I'm going deaf as well as blind," she said.

She glanced at her sewing basket and old sewing machine at the far end of the room. Unfinished clothes and the fabrics that she had worked on the night before were heaped up in the basket. Exhausted from working as a seamstress for over five years, she now felt her vision wasn't as sharp as before.

Since my mother had always given her best to any job she took on, even if it was a minor one, she was always busy with more orders than she could finish on time. Staring at the sewing machine, she seemed to be thinking that her arduous sewing, which often kept her working till midnight, was now even affecting her hearing.

Failing to open the front door and thus unable to enter the kitchen from outside, she decided to enter it through the door inside. After again tidying up her clothes, she opened the small door to the kitchen and then stepped down.

I quickly got up when I heard mother give a sharp cry. She was gasping as if frightened. And I knew that she had slipped and fallen down. But soon her gasping eased a little. Instead, her voice had changed and now sounded as if she was threatening something. But her fright made me think that it was my mother who was actually being threatened.

"Get out of here now!" Mother shouted, while stomping her heel on the kitchen floor—but her shouting lacked strength and wasn't menacing. I still didn't know whether it was a person or an animal that had frightened her so much.

"You little bitch, get out of here, right now!"

At that moment the hatch was suddenly flung open. When I saw my mother's flushed face, she shouted out in a firm voice,

"Bring me the rod!"

After hearing this, I quickly peeped into the kitchen before getting the rod from the shelf and handing it to my mother. And now her struggle began.

The person who had sneaked into our kitchen the previous night was a young girl and a total stranger to us. Mother gained confidence after realizing the intruder was a mere girl; her thrashing was harsh. But the girl didn't resist the flogging at all. It was clear to me that she was making a statement: she would bear the beating and wouldn't budge out of the kitchen.

But most of all what really scared me was that neither my mother, who was doing the beating, nor the girl, who was being beaten, shed any tears. It was my mother, though, who first became exhausted. Stopping her thrashing, she finally collapsed on the *bu-tu-mak*. Stricken by her chronic heartburn, my mother pressed her chest tightly with one hand and struggled to calm her rapid breathing.

I stole another look at the girl through the open door but couldn't make out her face clearly. And that was because, while resigning herself to my mother's beating, she was holding a dirty scarf around her face in order to protect it. Finally, Mother let out a long sigh and then said,

"Why are you doing this, you wicked thing?"

Judging by her height, she looked about three or four years older than me, sixteen or seventeen maybe. It was strange to see such a normal-looking young woman surviving by begging.

If she had to sneak into somebody's cottage and sit in front of their kitchen furnace to survive the cold, then that was understandable, but she should've left in the early morning before she was discovered. Being an intruder was bad enough, but once my mother noticed that she was a young woman, she exploded in anger and started whipping her.

Snowflakes slipped through the cracks in the kitchen door and sparkled like fluffy dandelion seeds. And the heavy snowfall striking the papered door sounded like somebody was hurling handfuls of sand at it. Staggering, as if buffeted by the whirling wind, Mother made her way to the main room. Her breathing was still rough. And her hands were trembling while holding her *jeo-go-ri* against her bosom.

All the while, it seemed that Mother didn't notice something that I had. A dried stingray, covered with soot and always hanging down from the kitchen doorjamb, had disappeared.

It was merely a dried fish, but to Mother it symbolized my father, who had left us when I was nine years old. Since the dried fish was hung on the doorjamb, my mother, regardless of her wanting to or not, saw it every morning and evening whenever she entered or exited the kitchen, and it always reminded her of my father. Once, when I still didn't know the name of the fish, I asked her what it was.

"I'm not sure, but I heard once that there's a bird living in the sea. It's a big bird, and it swims in the sea's depths, but people call it a stingray. And the ray-kite was named after it," she explained.

I nodded, since the shapes of the dried fish on the doorjamb and the ray-kite hanging on a rack in the room were indeed very similar.

Starting from the beginning of the year in the lunar calendar, I had flown ray-kites even after the year's first full moon. When I still flew kites after that, villagers would make fun of me and accuse me of being a rebel, but I ignored them and continued flying kites, as there weren't many other exciting things to do during the winter, and my knowing this helped me to ignore their jeers. So on windy days I always went out with my kite, and like a frog frolicking in mud, I jumped and ran up and down the embankment along the village stream.

Once I had released all of the kite's string and it was far away from me, appearing like a black dot sailing on the wings of the wind, my heartbeat quickened as the kite soared up and up, high into the sky. And my excitement was strong enough for me to totally forget the skin-piercing cold.

On those days I would often lose my kites, their strings usually snapping after becoming too taut when the kites soared so high. After the kites broke free, they would fly away over the mountain ridges, flapping up and down as they did, and I used to watch them vanish from my sight while feeling a great loss, and all this always reminded me of my father, who had left us behind a long time before.

Mother, though, didn't scold me at all for losing the kites. I often wondered, too, whether she knew about the paradoxical but pleasant sensations that I had experienced over my deep sense of loss.

To make me a new kite, Mother would always put away what she was working on. And even though she earned just enough to make a frugal living with her seamstress work, there was always material for kites. She began by picking up one of her paper patterns, piled up at the far corner of the room, and cut it to make a kite. Yes, whenever I lost my kite Mother always put her work away and immediately began to make me another without delay, and so I never needed to ask her to make me one.

And ray-kites were what my mother always made me.

After cutting a diamond shape out of paper, she glued two thin bamboo sticks, diagonally crossing each other, onto the paper. Following this, she bent a third stick into a semi-circle shape and placed it at the top of the diamond and then tied the two ends and the middle to the diagonal sticks. She then cut scraps of paper into thin strips and glued some of them at both sides of the kite to serve as ears and the rest she glued end to end to form a long tail, always much longer than an actual ray-fish tail. She finally attached one end of a reel of string to the mid-section of the kite where the two diagonal bamboo frames intersected.

Whenever Mother made kites, her face glowed with an enigmatic gleam. And I only realized much later that it was her way of waiting for my father, who at that time was leading a rootless, vagabond life.

Mother was known as a seamstress with such keen eyes that she was able to duplicate an outfit after only glancing at it on a person, and now I began to wonder how in the world she had missed spotting the disappearance of the dried ray fish from the doorjamb, even if she was in shock from the unexpected intruder.

Coming into the room, Mother sat motionless for a while, her eyes staring blankly straight ahead. After a long silence, she finally spoke.

"Well, what to do . . . it looks like there's no other way but to let her stay here until the snow melts away. And as they say, you've got to make sure there's a way out, even when you're chasing off an animal. You see, we're all trapped here in this heavy snow. But since a person and not an animal entered our house, I'm not sure whether this is good or bad."

Meanwhile, I had been stealing looks at the girl through the hatch opening. She was now squatting in front of the *a-gung-y*. Soon she picked up a poker and began probing through the ashes in search of hot charcoal.

After quite some time had passed, Mother went back to the kitchen. There she snatched the poker from the girl and drove her away towards the kitchen door and then made a fire, all the while remaining sharp-eyed.

I became anxious; it felt like my mother might, at any time, let out another scream. But contrary to this uneasy feeling, I heard no sound coming from the kitchen, except for the crackling flames and the twigs being snapped by my mother before she flung them into the furnace.

Located at the south foot of the Tae-baek Mountains, my village always had lots of snow in winter. When neighbors saw the signs of a big snowfall coming the night before, they connected their cottages with thick straw ropes. And the following morning, when the whole village was blanketed with snow, thick enough to almost level out the highs and lows of the world, the villagers, as soon as they got out of bed, would shake the ropes as a way of informing each other that they were okay. And then they would spend a good part of the whole morning shaking the ropes in order to make narrow passageways through the snow.

But the big snowfall we had that night was unexpected. And

even if we had anticipated it beforehand, Mother wouldn't have connected our cottage to the others anyway. Ever since my father left, Mother had withdrawn from people and wasn't willing to exchange labor with villagers or receive advice about anything.

It was obvious that my father's leaving greatly wounded Mother's pride. She therefore kept silent about the reason why he had left home and lived a rootless life, so much so that I didn't even know why he left. And for sure, Mother must've had a lot to say, but she never complained or even mentioned him at all.

Yes, she completely closed down. She also never shed any tears or expressed sorrow in an attempt to gain the sympathy of others. It must've been her fear of being disdained by her neighbors that made her behave like that. With an expressionless face, as if it was chiseled out of stone, she put all of herself into her sewing.

And she didn't look like she was trying to find my father, either. Because she had made kites for me every winter but never made an effort to fly any of them herself, it was clear to me that she would never look for my father but was just waiting for him to return by his own volition. But I knew that my father did in fact take up a large part of my mother's heart and that part had increased as time passed. And this I sensed through all her actions, especially when she made all the ray-kites without complaining and pretended indifference about my flying them.

Mother waited for her husband who had left her while I waited for my father who was invisible. She didn't tell me anything about him in order to keep her memories alive and pure within herself, and not knowing this, I too tried to keep alive my own memories of my father as much as I could.

"That hussy already filled her stomach. Last night she ate the whole fish in front of the furnace," Mother said from the kitchen.

"Did you know that it was missing from the beginning?" I asked.

"Do you really think I wasn't aware of it?"

"Did she say she ate it?" I asked.

"This girl stinks of fish, so what other proof do we need? It's as plain as the nose on your face. Do you think I thrashed her for no reason or because I wanted her to leave, all the while knowing that she had no place to go?" Mother said.

I heard water boiling and saw steam rising from the kitchen cauldron. Mother yelled out to tell me what she was about to do.

"Se-young, I'm going to bathe this girl, so don't look into the kitchen."

It didn't seem like my mother was thinking of my father that morning. She was preoccupied with the intruder and didn't have room in her mind for anything else, including my father. Mother turned her head around and glanced at me. She looked calm and relaxed. This made me believe that her fear and anxiety about the girl must've thawed while she was bathing her in the hot water.

Soon Mother came into the room, and after glancing at me, she quickly rummaged through the drawer for clothes. She took out a *jeo-go-ri* and a *chi-ma* along with some underwear that were all used but washed clean. And even when Mother stepped into the kitchen again I could still hear the girl washing herself. Before long, Mother called me to do a chore.

"Se-young, why don't you clear away some snow now?"

Stepping out of the kitchen with a shovel, I didn't know where to begin when suddenly facing the incredible amount of snow piled high everywhere. It seemed Mother didn't realize how useless shoveling snow was when it was falling so heavily.

As I expected, it turned out to be a dumb thing to do; all I did was scoop up snow from one side only to dump it on my other side, useless, just like my mother's efforts to chase the girl away, since the heavy snow had trapped us all together. And I was also afraid of being trapped alone, like a mole in the piles of snow. And if that ever happened, I knew I'd suffocate and die, die like a fish trapped in a small pond filled with moss. Obviously, I didn't want to shovel snow at all, so I pretended to do it, but actually, I was just scratching the snow's surface with the tip of the shovel.

From somewhere over the piles of snow, I heard people talking, but they were barely audible, and along with this, though coming from somewhere nearer, I also heard a dog barking. The people might've been inquiring if we were okay. I held up my shovel as high as I could and waved it in the air but didn't get any response.

Suddenly, my heart began beating and my body started trembling with fear. But I didn't want my mother to notice this, so I cleared my throat, trying to conceal my fear. Soon I realized she was preoccupied with the girl and had forgotten about me. From the kitchen I could hear Mother talking to her in a low voice.

"Where's your home?"

"I don't know," the girl answered, in a hoarse voice. Since sneaking into our kitchen, it was her first response to Mother's many questions. "Do you think I would be begging like this if my parents were alive or if I had a home?" she retorted.

She said this as if she was scolding Mother for asking such a question. Shaken by the girl's rude response, my mother half-smiled, half-frowned and then said, "Sorry, I didn't mean to upset you, but since we just met, don't you think we should at least know something about each other? What's your name?"

"I don't remember."

"This is ridiculous . . . wait a minute, what's the date today?" Mother asked herself.

It was then that she decided to call the girl Sam-rae. But the first name my mother thought of was Sam-lay. The day she came to our house was the night of the third day of December in the lunar calendar and thus Mother had first thought of Sam-lay, meaning "coming on the third day." But considering the girl's dignity, my mother changed the lay ending to *rae*, which means "decorum."

"People often say weeds are nameless, but there's no weed without a name. That worthless flower, the cockscomb, even has a name. And you, a human being, shouldn't drift about without one. This must be the reason you've been wandering as a beggar until today—because you didn't have your own name, a girl like you, who can speak clearly," Mother said to her.

At the time I wondered if she wanted to keep Sam-rae as a family member.

Mother had always suffered from a lack of helping hands. And this was because my father had left and she had to do all the housework, along with her sewing. Even in such circumstances she always kept a safe distance away from the village men and also hardly ever socialized with the village women. And she didn't take any medication for her chronic heartburn, either, as if it was a natural thing for someone to live with at least one affliction. But above all, there was one thing that my mother was strict about— my manners, since she didn't want me to be called a fatherless brat by the villagers.

Disregarding my discontent, my mother took the girl, now clean and no longer smelly, into the room. And it was only then that I realized my feet, deep in the snow, were freezing.

In the air above the distant, snow-covered field I saw snowflakes flapping like butterflies. And now and then I heard a dog barking, but I was unable to figure out from which direction it was coming. I soon dropped the shovel on the ground and sat on it.

Suddenly, the barking became louder. Upon reaching me, after running across the snowy field at full speed, the dog started licking my face and neck while wagging its tail wildly. It was Nu-rung-jy, meaning burnt rice, a neighbor's dog that always became overly excited whenever he saw me. His mouth smelled of fish and he kept madly licking my face as if trying to wear it away with his tongue. And his wagging tail even generated a mini snowstorm around us. It looked as if the dog had circled around our house in the snow for a long time and kept barking in an attempt to locate my whereabouts.

I hugged the snow-covered dog tightly and then finally gave him a light smack on his neck, signaling that he should leave now.

But ignoring my demand, the dog still hovered around me and didn't want to leave. My two legs were now buried deep in the snow.

"It looks like you need help clearing away all this snow. But as you know, everybody is struggling to clear up their own yard, so it won't be easy getting any help."

Hearing this, I turned around and saw Nu-rung-jy's owner, our neighbor Jang.

He and my father were very close friends. And since he lived right next door, he worried about me and came over to make sure I was all right. When I bowed, he approached me and asked, "Is your mother okay, too?"

"Yes," I said.

"This deep winter snow won't melt soon. But within three or four days we should at least have paths cleared between neighbors," he said.

Stumbling through the snow, I made my way to the kitchen door. Nu-rung-jy started to follow me and our neighbor didn't stop him.

When I spoke to Mother, who was still in the room, about what our neighbor and I had talked about in the yard, her face turned pale. Right then, Nu-rung-jy, who was growling while sniffing around the kitchen floor, got close to the hatch and then suddenly started barking, loud enough so that the kitchen ceiling might've collapsed. I scolded him, but he didn't stop barking. My mother then shouted,

"Se-young, get that dog out of the kitchen."

Stepping into the kitchen, Mother found a stick and raised it towards the dog. Nu-rung-jy quickly darted out like a gust of wind. But he soon jumped back in and was barking loudly while looking towards the room. It was obvious that the dog had sensed that a stranger was in there.

Because the dog repeatedly ran through the snow in the yard and in and out of the kitchen where Mother threatened him with the stick, a small path was created from the kitchen to the front yard.

I stepped outside. Under the eaves I found a ladder that was always there in case old roof tiles had to be replaced. Climbing the ladder, I struggled not to slide off and eventually reached the roof. An endless expanse of snow flooded my eyes. And the sky had just cleared and seemed to have sunk so low that I felt I could've touched it if I just stretched out my hand.

On the rooftop the snowflakes dazzled my eyes, as each of them reflected the sun's rays and glittered like delicate dandelion seeds. While wiping away the tears from the corners of my eyes, I shoved the snow off the roof. Our neighbor was now standing next to his fence with his arms crossed, looking up at me all the while. I soon sat on the roof's ridge.

From there I saw the embankment, where I usually flew kites, covered with thick snow and looking like a long shiny cumulous cloud. And at the edge of the embankment, the small ponds, once covered with blue bog moss, were now covered with snow.

I wished the snow-flies wouldn't spew out the bog moss that they had once swallowed. And I also wished that a stingray would swim around in the ponds, with enough oxygen to breathe, living happily ever after. Upon catching my breath, I climbed down the ladder.

Three days had passed since the snow had fallen, but it didn't seem like it was going to melt away easily. And this was because a cold spell had struck right after the big snowfall. But the calm and quiet air in our cottage returned. And I once again heard the sound of the sewing machine. The room was toasty warm, and whenever Mother handled new fabrics, their fresh smell hovered in the air. And now and then, when she stopped sewing, Mother and Sam-rae talked to each other in low gentle voices, and this added to the comfortable atmosphere in our home.

But ever since we had the heavy snow, Mother became more reclusive. She became somewhat cold and restrained, too, so much so that when Jang came with some other people and cleared the snow in front of our house, she didn't even greet them.

When she was done with the day's sewing, she put all her time into treating Sam-rae's frostbitten feet. Mother crushed the roots of lotus plants and shaped them into round paddies as big as her palm and then applied the paddies onto Sam-rae's afflicted skin after rinsing it with vinegar, or she boiled ginger roots and applied the liquid to the insteps of the frostbitten feet, repeating all this every morning and evening without any sign of being annoyed.

One foggy evening it was late enough to be dark, but in snow country the night didn't easily blacken. The village paths, brighter than they were in daylight, branched out atop the thick snow that had covered every corner of our village.

Sam-rae's frostbite was almost cured. She was peering into cottages in the village and I was reluctantly following her at a distance, making crunching footstep sounds on the frozen snow as I walked, when she suddenly turned around and signaled for me to come to her. She was heading towards one of the village's old thatched cottages.

Cottages each year had new thatched roofs added onto the old ones. So the older the cottage was, the thicker the roof was, with its eaves filled with holes like a rotten log—holes where birds made warm nests to survive the winter months. Since the eaves near the chimney were warmer, birds most often made their nests there.

Sam-rae and I sneaked close to the rear of the cottage. Early evening light glowed through a small paper window in an adobe wall as we focused our attention on the inside of the cottage, but we couldn't hear any sound. The family must've stepped out, leaving a light on. Realizing that no one was inside, we became bolder. Sam-rae stopped walking stealthily and I, without any reason, started giggling.

We headed towards the cottage's chimney and there Sam-rae squatted down in front of me. She then pointed to her shoulders, wanting me to get on them. The eaves were not that high up but still high enough so neither of us could reach all the way back into the bird holes. We may have reached the tip of the thatched eaves standing on our tiptoes, but since we couldn't reach the back of the holes, this would've given the birds enough room to escape and we would've fumbled our chance at catching them.

Having me mount her shoulders, Sam-rae struggled hard to stand up. And by trying to balance myself, I unintentionally was squeezing her neck with my two legs and covering her face with my hands, which didn't help matters. It was then that she shouted out, "You dumb country bumpkin, how can I see with my eyes covered up?"

Startled, I immediately took my hands off her face. This sudden move made Sam-rae stagger and miss a step, and as a result of this, I began thrashing my hands about in the air.

At that moment I saw another snow-covered world. In the silvery light that had even absorbed the night's sounds, I experienced a brief moment of feeling like I was flying above the snow.

The fresh wind brushed my forehead and entered deep into

my lungs, and this made me feel as if I had grown wings under my armpits, wings that were bigger and more transparent than those of a stingray. But the time when I felt I was flying was short lived, as Sam-rae soon began yapping, but nonetheless, it did feel like I had gone on an endlessly long flight over snow-covered fields.

"Hurry up. What are you doing?" she shouted angrily, while mimicking my village dialect.

Sam-rae glared at me with raised eyebrows. Teetering, she approached a hole in the eaves as I quickly grabbed onto the end of the roof. This helped her regain her balance and so now she was able to stand up straight. Without hesitation, I put my hand into the hole. Moving deeper into it, inch by inch, my hand was charged with a heightened sensation, but I didn't feel any bird. I became impatient. And a sudden fear swept through me.

It was right then that I felt something soft. It was not only soft, it was also squirming. Surprised to the point where my bladder almost burst, I quickly yanked my hand from the hole. I wondered whether I had touched a hibernating python or not.

Suddenly, when I saw something coming out of the hole, another razor-sharp fear shot through me. It was a small bird with its wings flapping. And soon it was wobbling while flying about in the air.

It flew straight across the snow-covered roof like a thrown stone, but then it plummeted down. Like a live shrimp bouncing on the ground, it tumbled about on the snow for a while before regaining its sense of direction and flying off towards the distant sky.

Captivated by the sight, we continued staring at the sky, but the bird didn't return. A sense of loss and regret, even stronger than I had experienced after losing a kite, rushed into my heart. It was the first time I truly realized that birds were flying animals.

"It's too bad we couldn't catch it, but the bird must be happy to be free," Sam-rae said to herself, with her eyes still gazing at the sky.

"Well, the father-bird flew away but for sure the mother-bird is still in the hole. Shoot, how dumb of me to ask you to catch it," she muttered.

My premonition that Sam-rae would get angry at me for not catching the bird and would smack me turned out to be wrong. Putting me down, she squatted on the snow instead and started peeing. The sound of her peeing was as sharp as the sound made when fabric was torn. Still squatting down, she told me, "Do you see the *ji-gae* over there? Bring it to me."

Leaning against the wall of the house, the *ji-gae* was half covered with snow.

Instead of having me sit on her shoulders, this time she mounted the *ji-gae* after leaning it against the adobe chimney. Spotting a hole, she scrupulously scraped away broken pieces of straw. Straw, black and rotten, fell down to the ground *en masse* and emitted a sour smell.

Sam-rae now pushed her arm deep into the hole, so deep that her armpit touched the eaves. It felt like a long time had passed without her catching a bird. But for sure, she was touching something and enjoying it. Finally, Sam-rae said to me,

"Take it. But don't hold it too tight . . . it'll die right away if you burst its heart."

Carefully, I held the bird with both hands. The bird was crying out. And its small, quivering body was almost too hot in my frozen palms.

"Give me the string," she ordered.

Skillfully, she tied the bird's foot to the end of the string.

"Now let it fly. Don't worry, it's not going to get away. And it will fly much higher and farther than any of your kites. And you'll see how much fun it is to fly a bird!"

But I kept on holding the bird in my hands.

"You hick, got scared, huh? Okay, if you can't do it, then go back home. Your mother probably thinks I've kidnapped you and is freaked out by now."

But when we arrived home with the bird, the only thing we heard was the sewing machine's familiar sound. Through the kitchen door opening I smelled almost-cooked barley in the cauldron. My mother usually showed little interest in what I brought home, whether kites or birds, but that night was different.

"Check on the barley. It should be done by now," Mother said to Sam-rae, while undoing the stitches sewn along a skirt's seam that she was dissatisfied with. With Sam-rae in the kitchen, Mother opened the back room's sliding door and said in a gloomy tone, "It's snowing again. You know, birds get their life from Heaven, too. Let it go! It's born with a quick-temper and won't eat any food you give it, and so it'll be dead within a few days if you keep it. Winged animals should fly freely. Yes, let it have its freedom, and let it die naturally after having lived a happy life."

She fell silent. Gradually and as usual, her silence made me feel uneasy. I didn't want to give her dumb excuses for being late, since I knew it would break the evening calm. So I decided to wait until she asked. But the tranquil night continued until late, and I only heard the sewing machine, nothing else. It was almost midnight, and I had already slept for three or four hours when my mother shook me awake.

I was still half asleep, my eyes barely open, when Mother pointed to the warmer side of the room. It was the spot where Sam-rae should've been sleeping, all curled up like a stray cat; it was the way she fell asleep, even when sleeping in a warm room.

"It's been quite some time since she left for the outhouse . . . and it seems she's gone," Mother said.

Yes, Sam-rae disappeared in the middle of the night. And

when I had to go out to find her, I didn't follow my mother's advice to track her footsteps. And that was because she didn't know how clever Sam-rae could be.

I discovered this when Sam-rae and I were about to take off for an evening of nest-raiding. Before we started walking, she quickly put on her rubber shoes backwards and then put me on her back. While she was walking, I saw her footprints behind us. As if cast in a mold, they were clear and looked as if one person had walked towards the house but no one had walked away from it. Once reaching the main road, she put me down and got her shoes on the right way.

But anyhow, it turned out that both Mother and I were wrong that night about how Sam-rae had disappeared.

Outside, atop the thick snow, I not only couldn't find any footprints of Sam-rae leaving, I couldn't even see any footprints of hers coming in. Compared to the previous snowfall, the snow that night was rather light, but I still didn't find any trace of her while walking all the way to the village's main road. Grey snowflakes were flying about in every direction. And it seemed that she too had just flown away. Like the bird whose nest I raided and who I chased out of its home, Sam-rae must've flown off to I didn't know where.

Judging by her smarts, something that enabled her to change two people's footprints into one person's, she must've also had the ability to fly over mountain ridges, like dandelion seeds.

Standing in the middle of the village, I thought of the countless kites I had lost. At those times, when my kites were flying away from me, their faces fluttering in the wind, I felt they were laughing at me.

I was at a loss about what I had to do. I didn't know where to go to find Sam-rae; it was as if I was up against a huge wall. But I knew that I had to try to find her. I became anxious, knowing there wasn't any place to go.

Like a wolf on a mountaintop, I held up my chin and looked at the sky. Just crying then would've been a simple thing to do. But that was a cowardly act for a thirteen-year-old boy.

Right then, I heard a gasping sound rushing towards me. Nu-rung-jy suddenly dashed in front of me and wrapped himself around my legs. But he was useless that night, as all the smells were long buried in the thick snow. Nu-rung-jy kept rubbing his snout against my trouser. And for quite a while, we stood there like that.

Tears ran down my cheeks, but my mind was calm.

The village in the middle of the night was so quiet, as if it had sunk into the earth. Maybe it was actually sinking beneath the bog moss in those ponds, I thought, sinking into the ponds that dotted the marshland, and there a stingray was swimming, with its flat head fluttering like wings. A stingray has such strong survival instincts that even three hundred meters down in the sea it keeps its eggs safely in a pouch called the mermaid's purse. This thought gave me hope that my father might still be safe and alive somewhere. Before long, I heard footsteps coming from behind.

"What are you doing here?"

It was our neighbor Jang, the man my mother didn't want to see. And since I had stood in the snow for a long time, it felt like all my bones were frozen and that it wouldn't be easy to turn quickly around to answer him.

"I was outside taking a pee and found that Nu-rung-jy wasn't home, thinking maybe a tiger might've taken him away, so I ran out to search for him. I must've scared you . . . did I?" said Jang.

"Yes," I answered.

"A boy your age who's always rushing about shouldn't have a problem falling asleep at night . . . so what made you come out here at this hour when it's snowing? Well, I think I can guess. You must be sad about your father having gone away, right? But what can you do but bear it as your mother does. If he didn't have that affair with the woman at the Springtime Bar, your mother wouldn't have to live the difficult life of a seamstress."

While listening to him, I heard Sam-rae's shout from behind.

"What are you doing here?" she asked.

I must've been gone a long time and so she finally began looking for me. Feeling fortunate to be rescued from my neighbor, I walked to Sam-rae, who was motioning in the distance for me to come to her.

"Why did you run away in the middle of the night?" I asked her.

"Stop talking nonsense. If I ran away, how come I was looking for you and I'm here now? Get home before you freeze to death," Sam-rae said.

"Don't you know that Mother will punish you if you keep lying like that?" I told her.

Between my mother and Sam-rae that night, no words were exchanged regarding her disappearance. While Sam-rae and I brushed off the snow from our clothes and went into our rooms and finally got into our beds, Mother had her head down and was engrossed in her sewing, her mouth sealed shut. And she didn't even explain how it happened that Sam-rae ended up looking for me that night.

Sam-rae's night trips continued in the following days. But whenever that happened, my mother didn't scold her or even say anything, but only gazed sadly at her. And in the mornings following her excursions, Sam-rae without fail would sleep late and look tired the rest of the day.

My mother finally realized that she was a sleepwalker. And there wasn't any way to treat it. It wasn't the kind of disease that could be cured with medicine. Furthermore, interrupting a sleepwalker would be a reckless thing to do. Therefore, Mother left her alone, knowing that if Sam-rae ever had a fit, her condition would rapidly become worse, not better.

"Children who live an unsettled life or who have experienced traumatic events while still young usually develop such a condition, but in most cases it disappears as they grow up . . ." Mother said to herself.

One night I heard Mother suddenly stop her sewing machine after working from early evening. Awake now, I was waiting for Sam-rae to open the back room's sliding door, since I was sure that she was preparing for her night's outing. But the door didn't open. Instead, I heard the main room's door to the porch open quietly. I saw my mother rising and stepping out into the porch, with her long skirt trailing over the doorsill. And she didn't come back, even after midnight.

I began counting numbers. I counted from one to five hundred, to one thousand, and then to five thousand, slowly, without skipping a number. I then gradually fell asleep.

When I got up the next morning Mother was firing up the kitchen stove to heat the room and was wearing the same enigmatic look that Sam-rae wore the many mornings she returned from her night outings. Finally, each of us now had a secret that couldn't be shared among us.

Like a buoy that never sinks into the water, even after years of being buffeted by surging waves, Mother never again hung another dried stingray on top of the kitchen doorjamb.

From the time Sam-rae had begun living with us, Mother often sewed all night because she began to get more orders. And Sam-rae was the one who made this happen. Also, whether I liked it or not, Sam-rae was now known as my cousin on my mother's side. Yes, even before my mother's realized it, Sam-rae had become an all-important companion to her. And this was a natural thing to happen, what with my mother being home all alone without friends after my father had left. Having a womanizer as a husband meant Mother also had to support us, and the only thing she could do was work as a seamstress.

While sewing, Mother frequently even skipped mealtime. Often I also heard her lamp wick sputter when it was running out of oil. And this wasn't all. Because of lack of sleep, she was also losing weight and her body got thinner as time went by. She often had hacking coughs and a swollen neck, too, and sometimes I saw her sleeping while leaning against the wall with sewing stuff in her hand. Occasionally, her thimble was soaked with blood after pricking herself while sewing.

But Mother didn't pay attention to her health at all. As if she had decided to die while sewing, she put all of herself into it, and sometimes she didn't even tend to her toilet in time. If such behavior wasn't coming from Mother's hatred towards my father who had abandoned her, she must've been hypnotized by Sam-rae. And before we were aware of it, Sam-rae was now the one who did all the house chores, both inside and outside, and she never made a big deal about it, either.

Like a stingray that has the marvelous ability to endure the water pressure three hundred meters below the sea, Sam-rae had the keen ability to spot and dig out the roots of wild lettuce buried deep in the snow covered ground. She also used to find goose grass or other herbs in the snow-blanketed ridges or in vegetable gardens and chew on them after they were rinsed clean in icy water. I knew those herbs helped people become less sensitive to cold weather.

Like a stingray that can still breathe through holes on its back when its body is partially buried in the sand at the bottom of the sea, I knew Sam-rae would survive even if buried in heavy snow. For this reason we weren't that different from the eggs of a stingray in Sam-rae's mermaid purse. And even though the eggs dreamt of hatching, there was little hope of escaping unless she opened her purse.

One night Mother accidentally discovered Sam-rae's real purse after she had left for her night trip. As her night-outings were now considered routine by then, Mother and I didn't worry about her absence at all but just waited for her to return.

Mother found the purse in Sam-rae's bedding that she must've dropped when she left. It was a silk purse with a purple morning glory embroidered on it, embroidered so delicately that it almost looked like a fine brush painting. And unexpectedly, the purse was filled with paper money, fifteen bills in all and of various denominations.

Mother woke me up and I noticed that her face was pale. After she told me what had happened, I understood well enough her disappointment. But having been bullied by Sam-rae ever since she came, I didn't want to defend her. Contrary to our expectation, though, Sam-rae soon returned. She directly went to her bedding, wearing her usual ambiguous expression, one that never revealed what was really going on with her.

Once she reached her bedding, her hands frantically searched through it, like the pincers of a mantis crab crossing over tidal mud in search of water, and when she came out from the other side of all her bedding, Mother realized that Sam-rae's sleepwalking must've ended a long time ago. Lifting up one side of her own bedding, Mother asked Sam-rae in a calm voice,

"Is this what you're looking for?"

Blushing like a red radish, Sam-rae glared at her purse in Mother's hand. But in an instant she snatched it away.

"Why do you have my purse?" Sam-rae snapped.

Her unexpected reaction made Mother's face once more lose color, and looking like she was having a heartburn attack, she almost hit her forehead on the floor where she was crouching down while grasping her *jeo-go-ri* against her bosom. But at that moment, while Mother was breathing heavily, Sam-rae threw her purse into the middle of the room, as if she no longer cared about it. She then quickly went to the kitchen and brought in a bowl of cold water for Mother. Hovering around, she acted amiably for a while, but regardless of this, the shock was too great for Mother to easily overcome, even after having drunk the water.

"Bring me a rod!" Mother told Sam-rae.

Sam-rae immediately stood up and went out and soon came back with two rods and placed them in front of my mother.

"Raise your skirt," Mother ordered.

Contrary to previous times, Sam-rae without delay obeyed my Mother like a lamb. She lifted her skirt up all the way, revealing her legs. It seemed to me that her beautiful white limbs were scorning my fuming mother. As soon as her legs were exposed, Mother shouted at me,

"Se-young, get away from here!"

Whenever the rod hit Sam-rae's calves, it was my mother not Sam-rae who let out a painful groan. But that day's whipping didn't last long. For some reason Mother flung the rod away early on. And instead, she began sobbing.

Sam-rae had finally ignited the wick of my mother's bitter sorrow, a sorrow that had been suppressed and had thus accumulated in her heart as time passed. And her sobbing, very restrained in order not to be heard outside, continued for a long time.

But Mother's weeping, which broke the night's silence, kindled a fear in me. And what I feared was that Mother might also leave home one night, as my father had done. And I could feel her hesitation and sadness about such a parting in her trembling shoulders and muted sobbing. Indeed, Sam-rae was the only one among us three who didn't show any fear at all. She soon turned away from my mother and was sitting facing the wall.

"Where did you get all this money?" Mother asked, in a nasal voice after sobbing a long time.

"The girls at the Springtime Bar gave it to me for taking their sewing orders," Sam-rae answered.

"So, you're saying the girls gave you tips, right?" Mother asked.

"Yes."

"I'll tear off your mouth if you're lying . . . do you hear me?"

"I'm not lying."

"I'm going to keep this purse for you. Do you have anything to say about that?"

"No."

But I didn't believe what Sam-rae told my mother, since I knew very well that she was very good at stealing.

Sam-rae had a place that she believed nobody knew about but her, and she hid things there. It was a hollow spot between the rocks in the backyard wall. She chose one of the holes in the wall that didn't get wet, even in a pouring rain, like those holes in the eaves, and there she stored trivial items.

She had a pair of white rubber shoes hidden there, and, like an owl's nest, they were stuffed with things. But they all looked useless to me, such as a copper ring, an old pendant, colored threads, a needle pouch, scraps of cloth, and a wrapping cloth that was folded up neatly, and all this was stored in the snow-white rubber shoes.

And I had found her secret spot but didn't tell my mother about it, as I didn't want to face Sam-rae's anger as a result of my squealing.

Even though Mother now had some idea where the money might've come from, she didn't give the purse back to Sam-rae. But, at the same time, she didn't hide it, either. Rather, she flung the purse to one corner of the room where everyone could see it and left it alone there for several days. Where the purse was thrown revealed to me the depth of the emotional chasm between my mother and Sam-rae.

Regardless of the sizeable amount of money there, Mother tried not to even glance at that corner of the room. The sense of betrayal she felt seemed to surpass the thickness of the purse. And this sense of betrayal consisted of two things: Sam-rae had hid the fact that her sleepwalking had ended in order to continue going out at night and that Mother knew she was preparing to leave us. But, nonetheless, Mother all the while didn't say anything about Sam-rae's ongoing night trips. Mother's distance in the matter could've been because she didn't want to face new pains or because the sense of betrayal she felt had put some distance between her and Sam-rae.

But Sam-rae was different from my mother. She acted as if nothing had happened. And so she continued going out at night, only not so often. During those nights when Sam-rae stepped out, her behavior was so bold and natural that both my mother and I wondered if her sleepwalking had returned.

My mother no longer asked me to follow Sam-rae on her night trips. Maybe she already knew that she wouldn't hear anything new even if I followed her. Whatever news I would've brought, whether about Sam-rae's sleepwalking returning or about her seeing some young man, would've upset her.

The following morning, when Sam-rae got up, Mother had her sit down and then said,

"From now on don't accept orders from the girls at the Springtime Bar. I was there last night and talked to them about it. The girls won't have to go naked because I stop making their clothes and we also won't starve because I don't get orders from them. Don't forget what I've just said . . . do you understand?"

Hearing that my mother visited the bar and knew about everything and feeling ashamed that she might know the truth, Sam-rae didn't go to the bar from that day on. And because of this, she soon became cheerless, different from before when she had bounced around in the snow-covered paths like a dancer. She now went out more often during the daytime and would wander alone on the ridges between the fields before coming back home. Mother's reaction to Sam-rae's behavior was distant, too. She didn't question her about her outings, either, whether they occurred during the day or night.

One day when my mother was out of the room for a while Sam-rae asked me,

"Isn't your father a womanizer?"

Surprised, I almost gasped.

"Isn't he?" she asked once more.

"What are you talking about? You shouldn't talk like that when you haven't even met my father. Don't you know my mother will punish you for saying that?"

"Hey, you dumb bumpkin, I know everything but I just don't talk about it. There's nothing I don't know," Sam-rae bragged.

"You beggar, you better stop putting on airs like that," I retorted.

Since Sam-rae spoke badly about my father without reserve, I couldn't restrain my words and so my tongue slipped when it shouldn't have. But Sam-rae turned the direction of our conversation towards something else without any visible signs of her being angry.

"I even know all the streets in a big city about one hundred twenty kilometers from here. I'm smart, huh? What do you know?"

It was about ten days later that Sam-rae disappeared from the village. No one saw her leaving. But there was a rumor circulating—one that couldn't be verified, though.

At the north end of the main road and next to a warehouse, there was a small bicycle repair shop. People could always see several rusty bicycles leaning against a wall that looked like it would collapse at any time. Not many went to the shop with any business, but people heard whistling tunes coming from there every day, all day long.

And this was more so when the village was covered with snow. A rumor had it that the young man who worked at the repair shop had taken Sam-rae to a nearby town on the back of his old bicycle. But Mother didn't bother to verify the rumor. Maybe that's because she had already expected such an event to happen.

Sam-rae's white rubber shoes were also gone from her secret spot. The night she disappeared, I recalled Sam-rae's purse and the embroidered purple morning glory on it that looked as fine as a brush painting.

Early the following morning, when my mother went to the kitchen to make breakfast, I heard her scream. Alarmed, I quickly ran into the kitchen and saw my mother pointing to the kitchen doorjamb.

There, where the dried fish had hung, I saw about half an armful of wild lettuce dangling. Sam-rae must've rummaged through the snow-covered ridges to gather them, and they were still fresh and green.

My mother seemed unable to turn her gaze away from the wild lettuce. She had a habit of chewing on that plant's roots during her frequent overnight sewing bouts, since its sap dissipated sleepiness.

When heavy snow fell that winter and stayed for a long time, the only person throughout the whole village who was energetic and filled with life was Sam-rae.

2

It was six years since my father had left home. And my mother's waiting without even bothering to find out his whereabouts continued, an uncompromising wait similar to when a snake coils itself up and doesn't budge.

After that winter passed when Sam-rae left, spring came again to the village. The raised paths between the rice fields that began at the foot of the mountains were covered with red Chinese milk vetch and the streams were filled with young carps and minnows with fleshy fins, swimming against the currents. Having just passed the winter, the minnows were very cautious and agile in their movements. After swimming very fast in the water, they would suddenly disperse in every direction or dash down the stream as fast as shooting arrows at the mere shadow of a passerby or a leaf bustling about in the wind.

The last third of May that year we rarely had any cloudy days and so the sunlight from early morning on would be as clear and dazzling as broken pieces of glass. And when the morning sun rose on its tiptoes above the mountain ridges, whose forest had been drenched by moonlight the previous night, and when a gentle breeze filled with the fragrance of young buds began stirring up the leaves of oaks and alders, cuckoos from distant mountains and male pheasants in the forest behind the village now and then broke the calm air of spring.

The cry of the male pheasants, ending after only two short

sounds, was completely different from those of other birds that were clear and lyrical. As if fear stricken, they would cast out these two abrupt sounds, and these sounds were infused with a deep yearning for their mates. But since no female pheasants responded, their passionate cries were fruitless.

In the morning during those days my mother, emaciated like a dried leaf, would sit on the front porch gazing vacantly at nothing in particular while basking in the sun and listening to the male pheasants in the mountain forest.

It wasn't easy for me to figure out why Mother paid more attention to the pheasants' cries than the cuckoos', echoing down from the distant hillsides. Maybe the pheasants' sounds reminded her of my father, who no doubt had a hard time surviving away from his village. She would calmly enter the room, dragging her heavy steps across the floor, and take a morning nap in order to rid herself of the fatigue accumulated during the previous night's sewing. With her *jeo-go-ri* tightly fastened, my mother's way of sleeping was very similar to Sam-rae's, whose huddled posture somehow revealed her deep-rooted, bitter sadness and strange readiness to wake up at any time and immediately run a long way. And this new and pitiful sleeping habit of my mother's began after Sam-rae had left.

Waking up from her morning nap, my mother's face would carry obvious traces of a yearning for my father, as though she was with him in her sleep. As with people who lack enough sleep, she often had symptoms of someone losing their memory, too. But once she combed her hair, her fatigue-drenched face disappeared and for a moment she beamed like a white gourd flower.

When my mother was taking naps in the morning, I oftentimes went to the village stream. There I liked to watch minnows that looked like fine handcrafted glass to me. For a long time I would squat next to the stream and watch the minnows swiftly swimming, and then the May sun, so sweet and bright, would shine upon me from behind and cover my eyes with its soft touch. And this was the beginning of my playing hide-and-seek with my sleepiness.

First I became languid for no reason and my eyelids felt heavy and then the water's surface that reflected the sun's rays gradually became hazy. Intermittently, I heard people talking to each other on the main road, a road with white poplar trees along its sides, the trees all looking like upside down brooms.

It was right then that I felt something nudging at my side, something that was also winking at me. Of course, I knew that it was caused by my sleepiness. I would then feel so light, as light as dragonfly wings, so much so that I wouldn't have registered any weight on a scale. This enabled me to fall asleep while resting against the sunlight rather than the sunlight resting against me.

Squatting by the stream, where dandelions and wild asters were budding out of the earth, I enjoyed the drowsiness, drowsiness that became stronger as I tried to overcome it, while my mother was napping in her room, curled up on the floor where so much fabric was piled up that it could've covered up a rainbow. Springtime returned, weaved with drowsiness and stories of waiting. We waited for someone to visit us, anyone, and it didn't have to be my father.

As we began to sense that little hope was left of my father returning and as we realized that all our waiting might be in vain, we began to wait for somebody else to arrive. It would've been good if Sam-rae, who had come during that outrageous snowfall and left after living an outrageous life with us, had come back or someone else had shown up.

Living all by ourselves in the mountain village for so long, it seemed my mother and I had lost our sense of direction. And this made us feel that we were helpless, so much so that we didn't feel capable of even finding somebody to be with; no, that person would have to come to us. But my mother and I had never openly revealed this secret wish to each other. To admit that we were eager to be with anyone, even a stranger, was something we just couldn't easily talk about. But it was Sam-rae, a stranger, who had left us with a lasting sense of loss. She, though, had also left us with so many memories and colorful experiences.

Even old things look new if you look at them with fresh eyes. With this truth, memories of Sam-rae were meaningful, something that had enriched our monotonous lives, where the only thing that stirred up the air was the sewing machine operating. And this contributed to my mother and me harboring the illusion that Sam-rae was still living with us.

At sunset, when the western sky glowed red, I used to stand on the embankment and watch myself seemingly turn transparent, as transparent as a cicada's just-hatched caterpillar, while being saturated by the sun's warm rays. At those times I became like a sea sponge, absorbing the stillness of the splendid red sky into my heart, a stillness that almost melted my whole body. But no one in the village recognized the naked me. And right there on the embankment, whenever I wanted, I could meet my father, regardless of how far away he was from me.

My father always emerged from the western side of the embankment, with the sunset reflecting on his back. He appeared first as a small figure slowly approaching me until he passed by and finally disappeared at the eastern end of the embankment with his back to me. I could clearly see his features at those times, though he wasn't aware of my staring at him. Of course, my memory of what he looked like wasn't that accurate. But, nonetheless, he bore clear evidence that he was indeed my father.

Whenever I saw him he was holding a familiar ray-kite in one hand that I had lost on the embankment. And in the other hand, which was as cracked as the bark of an apricot tree, he was carrying a thin staff that looked as if it would easily snap if he ever made a wrong move. He was also limping heavily and trembling while walking and this made me wonder what exactly was ailing him.

He appeared to be putting more weight on his staff than he needed to, and so his shoulders jerked up and down whenever he took a difficult step. Moreover, when passing by me he tried to walk naturally, as if wanting to show me that he wasn't limping, but this only increased his pain, to the point where his face would contort. But all his efforts only made his appearance more miserable.

As far as I remembered, though, my father didn't have any of these physical conditions. But regardless of this, he always appeared to me as a limping man with a cane. Maybe it was my old feeling of having been betrayed by my father, who hadn't contacted us for almost six years, which made me envision him as a wretched and tortured figure.

Another winter came. Mother and I were waiting for a winter like the previous year, but none of us spoke about it. One night, in the middle of November, we had the first snow of the year, but it wasn't as heavy as the year before. That night Mother opened the door and stared vacantly at the gray night sky while saying to herself, "There must be a place in the sky where only snowflakes live."

Sitting behind her, I was also watching the falling snow when I told her, "Mother, I heard that the snow country isn't in the sky. They say that there's a place called Nepal, a mountain country, where only snowflakes live and nothing else, and there a king rules only snow."

"Don't talk nonsense. Look, snow's falling from the sky, and I've never heard of any mountains higher than the sky," said Mother.

"If there are mountains where only snowflakes live, then there should be mountains higher than the sky," I said, "and I heard these mountains are called Himalayas. I heard that once winter comes there, snowflakes ride the winds and drift down to the sky and wander about before falling to the earth and returning home."

"Where are those mountains?" Mother asked.

"I heard they're tens of millions of miles away," I said.

Mother stopped asking questions. Instead, she was silent, watching the snowflakes and cherishing each of them, snowflakes that were dancing gently downward in order not to hurt their delicate wings against the ground that was just beginning to freeze.

Her face didn't show that she remembered the hardships we had experienced during the previous year's heavy snow. It was clear to me that Mother also had been waiting for this snow. Chilly air was now beginning to hover in the room and my hands became cold, but Mother, looking as if she wasn't aware of it, lamented, in a barely audible voice, "Even snowflakes, living tens of millions of miles away, never fail to find their way back every winter, but your father must've become blind long ago. Unless he's lost his sight, how come he's unable to return to the home he left with his eyes wide open?"

From the beginning of that winter Mother began making patchwork cloth-wrappers instead of ray-kites. She used scraps of fabric that looked like baby palms to make the wrappers.

Rummaging through scraps of fabric in a basket that she hadn't touched for a long time, she took out some pieces and sewed them together, end to end. With her heart totally in it, sewing one piece after another was a tedious and lonely job with no end in sight.

Whenever there was time between sewing orders, she took out a cloth-wrapper and worked on it. The wrappers reminded me of terraced rice fields along mountain slopes and gave me the impression that Mother was turning her heart and time, which had been speeding directly towards my father, into a twisted spiral.

Mother not making ray-kites any longer and her being so absorbed in making the cloth-wrappers was, on the surface, a big change. Her poignant yearning for her husband, though, didn't disappear but continued to grow, only now it was festering inside her heart.

She must've known that keeping everything inside her would be much more painful, but regardless, she had chosen to do so. It was about mid-December when she finished two cloth-wrappers that were soaked with her heart-rending coughing and stained with her dried teardrops.

It happened one day at sunset when the remaining snow from the November snowfall dotted the earth that I saw Jang waiting for me in front of our gate. I was about to utter a casual hello and pass him by, but with his chin, he motioned me to the end of our alleyway.

Once we got there, he lit his cigarette and held it between his lips. He then took a couple of puffs, but he still didn't say a word. Soon, though, he alluded to the fact that Sam-rae had reappeared in town.

Coincidentally, the day I met Sam-rae again was the night we had our second snowfall of the year.

I saw her at an ordinary-looking house in town, one without any sign on its gate or under its eaves. I had already been in town several days before I met her, just roaming about, but it wasn't the kind of place where drinkers moved in and out or women's congenial laughter was heard. And so, I didn't even imagine that Sam-rae would be living in that house.

What made it possible for me to see Sam-rae there was the snow we had that night. I was walking and approaching the house located at the end of an alleyway when I saw two women watching the snowfall through a wide open door.

Like caressing hands, lamps lit their alluring figures, figures of women clothed in *han-boks*, consisting of beautiful *chi-mas* and *jeo-go-ris*.

Like fishing boats moored at a harbor with their many flags flapping in the wind, the room flickered before me whenever the wind rose. But when the wind calmed, the room reminded me of a fish tank containing colorful tropical fish, fish floating motionless in the water and lit by showering lights.

The two women were right behind the doorsill and were watching the snowfall in the yard when suddenly one of them rose and stepped onto the porch. I then recognized that it was Sam-rae. I was so surprised that I felt my heart would burst. It didn't take long for her, while holding her *chi-ma* up in one hand, to step down from the porch and walk across the yard to the gate. Once outside the gate, she held one side of her long skirt between her chin and neck and then lowered her rear end near the ground and urinated in the snow, unabashedly. I stole a quick look at her snow-white buttocks. It was after she had pulled up her underwear from her ankles that she spotted me.

"Is that you, Se-young?" Sam-rae said.

After seeing her buttocks, it was I, not her, who was surprised. She spoke so naturally, without any sign of feeling ashamed, that I wondered if I heard her correctly. She motioned to me, saying, "Come over here."

I stood there hesitating for quite some time. Finally, she came to me as I crushed the snow with my foot, not knowing what to do. She stared at me from every angle and then in a stern voice said,

"A young boy like you shouldn't come to this kind of place."

She was chewing gum and her breath smelled of peppermint.

"Noo-na," I called out. It was so natural to say and my first time addressing her so warmly by calling her an elder sister. But no more words came out of my mouth. Sam-rae, though, didn't acknowledge such a change in me. Never mind acknowledging it; she didn't even show any sign of noticing anything.

"You must've heard rumors about me and that's why you're here, right? But it's none of your family's business now. That's all in the past. Stop making yourself pitiful in this snowfall and go back home," she said, coldly.

"Noo-na, it's not so," I said.

"Whatever you say, I don't care. So stop roaming about here and get lost!" she said.

She was as cold as ice. Holding up one end of her *chi-ma* so as not to get it wet, she went back into the fish tank.

On the way back home I kept thinking of what she had said—"Get lost!"—but I couldn't understand why she had said it. My heart was heavy at such indifference coming from Sam-rae, who didn't show any sign at all of remembering anything from the previous winter.

But I had a passion flaming inside me and this quelled everything, quelled the strangeness I felt from her fantastic transformations, quelled her indifference and scorn and anger. So I, regardless of what she had said, returned home rather lightheartedly.

And it was one afternoon after three days had passed since I saw Sam-rae that I again met Jang, who told me that he knew exactly where she was. He was waiting for me in front of his gate with his dog.

"Have you asked around about the girl?" he inquired.

"Yes, I have," I said.

"So you managed to find her without my help . . . good. But finding her isn't good enough—something should be done about her," he said.

"Yes," I replied, rather vaguely.

"It can't be something that difficult. Maybe she doesn't have any traveling money to leave town, and if that's the case, I would like to lend her some money, since your father and I are more than just friends, we are like brothers. But if I did it, your mother would probably speak ill of me and say I'm butting into other people's business," he said.

"I understand," I replied.

"So you now know why I don't get directly involved in this situation. Anyway, it should be taken care of early enough before the whole village knows what she's doing in town. And you should remember that you're the man in your family now and are responsible for matters in your house, get it?" he said.

"Yes," I answered.

Absentmindedly, I gazed at the dismal village cottages and at the distant mountain ridges that revealed their dim shapes under the winter's gray sky.

"Stop just saying 'yes' and do something about it. You're old enough now to take care of matters like that. You must know your mother well, a lady with such a keen sense that she can distinguish pine needles from oak leaves by just hearing their falling sounds. You better work on it before she gets to know about this matter. It's disgraceful to have a young relative working as a bar girl," he said.

"Do you really think that my mother will make a big deal out of it if she finds out?" I asked.

"Of course she will. You must know by now that for the last several years your mother has been extremely cautious not to provoke any gossip about her life without a husband, as cautious as if she was walking on thin ice," he said.

That night I went to town to see Sam-rae. As I was leaving home, I cooked up an excuse for Mother and told her I was visiting a friend in town.

"It's nice that you have a friend in town now," she said, smiling and looking satisfied. But I didn't miss a fleeting shadow crossing her face. She didn't seem to notice, though, that I was lying to her.

Arriving in town, I went to the tavern and squatted down on the ground against a mud wall in the alleyway. And whenever I felt cold, I lit matches. It was overcast and dark, too, but I wasn't afraid.

With my hands under my armpits, I endured the cold while looking up at a starless sky. And since it wasn't snowing that night, I couldn't expect Sam-rae to again run impulsively out of the house to take a pee in the snow. But I just couldn't leave the spot.

Like gushing dam water, now and then women's uproarious laughter burst from the house. Whenever this happened, the darkness that filled the whole alleyway undulated like wine in a barrel, and out of this swaying darkness, a condor, with a white feather-ring around its neck, appeared in the sky above. It looked as if the bird was swept away by a tornado while flying above the Andes Mountains and was now circling low within my view.

With its aquiline nose pointing upward, this bird of silence continued to orbit above the tavern. I imagined that it could easily smash the fish tank by merely flapping its wings and then scoop up Sam-rae with its strong talons. This fantasy offered me solace and enabled me to forget the coldness that was actually piercing my body.

In no time I turned into a condor and was now flying freely in the night's overcast sky. My body was equipped with long thick feathers that protected me from the gale and cold.

Passing through low clouds, I soared high up into the sky. In an instant I was riding the wind with my feathers blowing, flying towards some unknown destination. Before long, I saw something, but since my eyes were dazzled, I didn't clearly recognize it at first.

I soon made it out—it was the snow kingdom. Standing on top of a snow-covered mountain at the edge of the sky, the kingdom's palace shone like a gemstone. What was shining, though, wasn't only the palace. Fearless snowstorms, swirling like a whirlwind around the palace, were also shining brightly.

I, for the first time, realized that a snowstorm could produce roaring sounds, menacing enough to churn up the earth by merely twisting about. Without stopping its gyrations, the snowstorms rushed in at full speed towards where I had just fled from. I now knew, as my mother and I had hoped since winter began, that a heavy snowfall would soon arrive at the village.

It was right then that I heard a voice.

"I knew something like this would happen. I had a hunch about it since early evening."

It was Sam-rae. Dispersing the darkness, she appeared in front of me and approached close enough for her nose to almost touch mine, and I then clearly saw her eyes glaring viciously. She seemed to be very upset at my being there. Revealing her white teeth that resembled a densely arranged corncob, she spoke scornfully to me while I timidly kicked the earth with the tip of my shoe.

"You hick, what made you come here again and pester me? Did your mother ask you to do this?"

"Oh no. Mother doesn't know anything," I said.

"Why then are you loitering here like this? Do I owe you any money?" she snapped.

"No, no, nothing like that," I said, faltering.

"Then tell me why you're here again," she snarled.

I took the matchbox out of my pocket and lit a match. I drew the match light close to her face. The darkness that had soaked into her face gradually disappeared, and a fully bloomed, yellow poppy flower appeared in front of me.

It was the legendary beautiful flower that blooms only once a year, a lofty yellow flower that only reveals itself to a person yearning for it. But at that moment, biting words struck my ears like a hammer.

"Put the light out, you idiot!"

As the match's tip, burning like a tantalizing red mulberry, gradually lost its color, the feathers of darkness, which had temporarily withdrawn, rushed back like a swarm of dayflies, and with this, the yellow poppy flower also vanished.

Disregarding what Sam-rae had to say, I kept striking matches, one after another, each of which bloomed a beautiful but sad yellow flame. And this mysterious atmosphere created by the match flames brought back memories of the time I spent with her, memories that were fading away.

But soon I noticed that Sam-rae was staring silently at me with her mouth tightly sealed. When I finished lighting the eighth match, she suddenly held my wrist and gently said to me, "You must be very cold."

"No, I'm not," I answered, shaking my head. Sam-rae gazed down at her shoes for a moment or two.

"You wait here for a second," she said. She scurried away into the fish tank while lifting up her long skirt, as beautiful as the fin of a tropical fish, but soon she rushed back out. She then spoke to me in a more concerned voice, "It's late now. What if, while walking without any matches, you come across a pothole on the road and fall in?"

While saying this, she gave me a new matchbox packed with matches reeking of sulfur. Yes, it was a cloudy night and so the road home was very dark. But I could get home without using even one match from the new box.

Since it was unusual for me to step out at night and stay out late, especially during bitter cold nights, my mother looked suspiciously at me when I came home after seeing Sam-rae. But she approached the matter very cautiously. She didn't directly question me about anything and simply asked, "Se-young, would you hold the other end of this?"

She was finishing a wrapper and was about to hem the edges.

And this is the step where she needed someone to hold the other end, otherwise the hemming would be uneven and squiggly, like the path of an earthworm on the ground. I knew, though, her intention was also to have a close look at me while I helped her. Holding one end of her wrapper, my hands were shaking. It was caused by the coldness that had penetrated into my bones while walking outside and that now was seeping out of my skin in the warm room.

"Do you know that you're acting a little strange lately?" she asked.

I felt my heart throbbing violently, but I shook my head.

"It's obvious that you've been acting oddly. Your eyes resemble those of a young widow who's lost her husband in a war—they're unfocused and drifting. And this isn't something I can ignore," she said.

"I don't know what you're talking about, Mother," I responded.

"Look at you, acting like a man of the world, evading the point. It's suspicious," Mother insisted.

Two days later it snowed again. Being naturally shy, snow always fell during the night and thus people could only see her figure in the morning.

Because of Nu-rung-jy's barking and the scratching sounds he made on our gate, I managed to wake up early that morning. Opening the door, I saw the whole yard covered with snow. And after searching for food in the snow, Nu-rung-jy's snout was all white. Bewitched, I gazed for a while at the ocean of snow that unfolded in front of me. *How come snow combines coldness and warmth, emptiness and fullness, scarceness and abundance in full harmony?* I wondered. It was a magic feat that only snow falling in a mountain village can perform. Under the snow-blanket, everything coexisted in a harmonious oneness.

After dinner the following day, Mother unexpectedly began changing her clothes. As if her head was full of thoughts, her moves were unhurried, and when she was finally done, she told me,

"You're going with me."

It was totally unexpected, but I knew exactly what was on her mind. Both my mother and I had this ability to quickly read each other's thoughts. Before I asked her anything, she said, "We shouldn't leave the cottage empty for too long. Let's get going and come back as soon as possible."

Hastily, we left home. Snow lightly covered the road and the moon was bright in the sky. Without lighting any matches, we walked quickly towards town.

Even though my father hadn't departed for the other world, Mother when going out always stubbornly wore white clothes like a widow. In a snow-white *chi-ma* and *jeo-go-ri* and full of energy, she vigorously walked on the moonlit road, and soon I smelled an odor coming from her sweaty back. Swinging her arms spiritedly, she strode on her way, and it was right then that I swear I saw wings under her armpits. Mother's white sleeves flapped like bird's wings as she moved briskly along the road that was flanked by poplars on both sides.

I realized that not only the *jeo-go-ri* Mother was wearing that night but also all the other *jeo-go-ris* that she had tailored for her clients were all soaked with her strong yearning to fly away, fly away like the fairy in a folktale who became a woodsman's wife after losing her celestial *jeo-go-ri*, one that she needed to fly back to her heavenly palace. I then also thought that maybe Mother's old yearning was the same as mine.

Maybe we were heading towards the snow palace in the far away snow country. Or maybe we were flying towards the city where my father was living. With Mother walking ahead of me, we soon passed the Springtime Bar located at the town's entrance.

When we reached the beginning of a street where a dried-seafood store was located, I stopped walking and cleared my throat. I did so with the intention of letting Mother know that she had just passed by the store without stopping. Sensing my intention, she turned around but her eyes were icy cold. After giving me such a cold gaze without saying a word, she kept walking towards the town's main road. That night on the road she wasn't the same woman who was always exhausted from sewing and often fell asleep peacefully with her hand on her chest.

When Mother entered the now familiar alleyway, I felt that my feet weighed tons. But when she finally stopped near the tavern, I suddenly felt a strange lightness. *How did she find out that Sam-rae is working here? Was it Jang who told her about it? Or was it one of the village women who rarely came to our house?*

I was dying to know how Mother found out that Sam-rae worked there, but it wasn't something that I could ask her in the middle of the alleyway. Mother got us a room from an old woman living near the tavern. The room was dimly lit by a wick dipped into kerosene that filled a small tray. With all of its contents revealed, the tray appeared to be a gutted carp that had floated to the surface of the village swamp. Feeling somewhat miserable, I was looking at the tray when Mother told me, "Go and bring Sam-rae here."

She ordered me as if everything about Sam-rae was under my control. I was dumbfounded by her obduracy and cantankerousness. But there wasn't anything for me to do but to obey her. Getting out of the house as quickly as I could, I ran towards the tavern. I thought that regardless of the outcome I had to inform Sam-rae that Mother was there and this quickened my pace. When I arrived at the tavern I didn't wait for her outside as I usually did.

Entering the yard, I saw the lit room and called out for Sam-rae. The fish tank was undulating with alluring lights tinged with nocturnal pathos, and soon its door flung open and Sam-rae appeared in splendid clothes, looking like a beautiful tropical fish.

She was so surprised that she almost let out a cry. She must've never imagined that I would go there and call out her name in such a roaring voice, since she appeared intimidated.

Fixing her eyes on me, she walked slowly across the front porch before stepping down into the yard. Once close to me, she grabbed my shirt collar and dragged me out of the yard. She loosened her grip only after I said, in a choked voice, that Mother was nearby. After that, we just sat side by side against the wall.

She soon took out a handkerchief from her *jeo-go-ri* sleeve and wet it with her spit and began quietly removing the makeup from her lips and cheeks.

"Noo-na, don't wipe your makeup away," I said, softly.

"Why?" she asked.

"Well, just don't," I said.

She remained silent for a moment and then said gently, "No, it's not right to see your mother with my makeup on."

We sat there gazing at the sky. Studded with stars, it looked particularly high and vast that night.

"Did you know that stars take shits at night?" she suddenly asked me.

I jeered.

"Nonsense! Stars don't take shits," I said.

Bursting out with a sudden anger, she said,

"You idiot, a fourteen-year-old boy still doesn't know that? If the stars don't take shits, why do we see stars shitting down at night like birds?"

She was saying preposterous things at such a tense time. But soon she rose and brushed off the dirt from her skirt and said in a barely audible voice, "No bastard can dare tell me what to do or what not to do. I'm on my own. But how strange . . . why do I lose my nerve in front of your mother. I wish she'd take a huge diarrhea shit like the stars," she said.

We slowly walked down the alleyway. Entering the main road, I pointed to the old woman's house and from then on Sam-rae walked in front of me.

While sitting down right across from my mother, with the lamp between them, Sam-rae, without uttering any greeting, fixed her gaze at Mother but avoided her eyes. The two women, sitting facing each other over the dim light, looked miserable and cheerless. Seeing Sam-rae sitting across from Mother, I left the room and closed the door behind me and then squatted down on the porch. A heavy silence hovered inside the room, but any sobbing sounds that I had expected didn't materialize. Not hearing any sobs coming from the women, I was disappointed. It was Mother who spoke first.

"I'm not sure but I can imagine why you returned to the place you once left. And of course, you must've had a reason to do so. I know, too, that as a woman you've already done irreparable damage to yourself."

Mother's voice was soft, but it was poignant enough to prick Sam-rae's heart. And it was something that Sam-rae had to listen to, whether she wanted to or not. I waited and wondered how she would respond. But what she said was something unexpected.

"Se-young, come inside!" she called out.

"Wherever he is, it's none of your business," Mother said, sharply, attempting to stop her from saying anything further.

"So you don't mind if Se-young freezes to death?" Sam-rae retorted.

"Freeze to death or not, it's not your business," Mother said.

"You've just said what I want to say to you, but I won't. Se-young is outside in the cold because of me. Don't you care if he freezes to death?" Sam-rae asked.

"If you listen to me and do as I say, we'll leave here before he dies," Mother said.

"What do you want?" Sam-rae asked.

"There's no time to waste. Leave this town immediately by any means. You know that the villagers believe that you're my relative, don't you? And you must know that I would be laughed at if I tell them now you're not. They don't know anything about you and me and will think that I've disowned my relative because she works in such a disgraceful place. If I had even one single woman in my family like you, I wouldn't say a word to you, even if I had ten mouths, but I don't have any one like you disgracing my family's reputation. If what you're doing is shaming someone's family, a family that has nothing to do with you, don't you think it would be the right thing to leave as soon as possible?"

"I've never said that I'm your relative," Sam-rae retorted.

"That's right. It was me who made up the story about our relationship. But I didn't know then that I would be dealing with this kind of situation. And the reason I said you were our relative was because I didn't want the villagers creating tales about you and us. You must've known this, and that's why you left without saying a word. If you ever thought of me as a relative, you wouldn't have left like a lost calf, would you?"

I was shivering. The cold, which I hadn't felt as much when waiting for Sam-rae outside the tavern, was now penetrating my skin and constricting my whole body. But I wanted this bitter cold to enter into me and to painfully gnaw at my bones. I wished that my body would finally freeze up like that of a pig hung on a butcher shop's rafter, frozen solid right to the intestines, frozen to such a degree that I would never be able to recover, even after the whole village becomes topsy-turvy in its effort to save me.

I wished that my body's shivering would become more and more severe and produce rattling sounds in the porch that would be heard inside. I loosened my tight grip on the lapels of my jacket, a grip I had kept in order to ward off the cold. And now my whole body was shivering terribly.

It was right then that Sam-rae said, "If you let Se-young come in, I'll tell you whether I'll leave or not."

"You don't need to worry about him. He's not so weak that he'd die in this kind of weather," Mother snapped.

I entered the room as if I was forced to and sat down. Sam-rae briefly glanced at me. And I saw that her eyes were teary.

"Don't worry, I'll leave," Sam-rae said.

At that moment, Mother put her hand inside her skirt and took out a money pouch. As Sam-rae and I watched, Mother counted out over twenty high denomination bills. I could see that she had kept only relatively new bills. She then bound the money with a rubber band.

"I'm sad, too. But what can we do? I'm sorry, but you need to leave this place, otherwise our village will be flooded with rumors about you, and Se-young will continue being restless and agitated and my life would be without peace," said Mother.

She then quietly drew Sam-rae's hand close to her and slipped the money bundle, hard as a rock, into it.

"Pretend you don't have this money and forget about it, but when you meet a situation where you think you really need it, then use it," Mother told her.

Taking the money, Sam-rae only gazed at the lamp wick and avoided looking at Mother. But she didn't shed any tears. Mother got up and told me, "Well, you must be warmed up enough by now, Se-young. Let's go."

The three of us left the old woman's house. Mother put me in front of her and hurried my steps so that I wouldn't have a chance to turn around and look at Sam-rae. Once on the road, she quickened her pace. Nu-rung-jy, who had followed us and had waited outside the alleyway, was right behind us.

In the darkness the snow-covered road we had taken on the way to town now stretched out before us once more. Not long afterwards, we left the main road and began walking towards our village, which seemed to be floating above the foot of the distant mountain, when Mother suddenly began having a coughing spasm. Grasping a white poplar tree, she was coughing as if she was spitting out her guts, all the while struggling to calm herself down. I kept looking, though, at the embankment running along the village.

"Se-young, let's stop for a break," Mother said.

Still holding her *jeo-go-ri* against her bosom, she sat on a pile of stones alongside the road. Fixing my gaze on the embankment that lay east to west, with its ends blurry in the dim night's light, I wished for a splendid sunset-glow to appear in the sky. But contrary to my wish, the embankment remained covered by the night's gray light and not by a red glow. Still, I felt that if I wished hard enough, the glow would push away the night's gray light and flood the earth with red.

I waited and waited but such magic didn't happen. Never mind the magic, the wild plants disappeared from my mind, plants like wild lettuce and whitlow grass that I had often seen blooming in the snow on the embankment. They were dear to me, such trivial things in such ordinary places, but now they had all vanished. Tears welled up in me. And I soon heard Mother's sorrowful monologue coming from behind me.

"If I didn't have you, I would've followed Sam-rae and left. Like hers, my mind has always drifted like a cloud. But how strange, my mind is now cloudless. The money I gave Sam-rae was what I had saved for your father whenever I got paid, selecting only new bills, too," Mother said.

I sat behind her, with my back to hers while furtively wiping my wet eyes with my shirtsleeve.

"But since I gave the money to Sam-rae, I'll no longer have any excuse to have dazed dreams at night or to float on clouds anymore. I now won't be able to even think of taking off to where your father is, even if I find out where he lives, but my mind's never been this light, so much so that I feel I could fly to the sky. Yes, the money finally went to where it belongs. And I'm now free of holding a grudge, and Sam-rae will use the money as her fate decrees," said Mother.

Finally, she began crying. Not long afterwards, she took off her silk scarf, with which she had wiped away her tears, and put it around my neck and said,

"Let's go home. The night is deep. Even the Milky Way isn't in the sky tonight."

That night Mother asked me to sleep in the main room. She slept on the warm part of the floor and I on the other side next to her sewing machine. As she had said, she must've felt lighthearted, for she fell asleep as soon as she laid herself down in her bedding.

I listened to her peaceful breathing. It was a contagious sound that could also induce sleepiness in a listener, but I couldn't fall asleep. What preoccupied me were Sam-rae's eyes, which had glanced at me as she entered the tavern's alleyway after having left the old woman's house.

It was such a brief glance, and I wondered what she wanted to communicate by it. I thought about it, over and over, but I couldn't figure out anything that would satisfy my heart.

And as a fourteen-year-old boy, I just wished that I were more mature and old enough to know what it was all about. But eventually, I fell into a deep slumber.

When I woke up the following morning, I noticed that I was lying down on the warm part of the floor where Mother had slept and Mother was now where I was before, the cold spot. It was early, and in the dim room I opened my eyes while still lying down and saw that she was facing the wall and resting on her side, her thin back facing me.

I was so moved by her caring that tears ran down the sides of my nose. She already knew that I had to let go of Sam-rae and that parting from her broke my heart.

I tore sheet after sheet of paper from a thick blank notebook and, with my pencil wet with my spit, I began drawing Sam-rae's face on each page, but I couldn't clearly capture her, so even after half the notebook was used up, I still wasn't content with my drawing. I then knew that I wouldn't be able to draw a face resembling hers even if I used up ten notebooks.

It was because what I called a "drawing" was nothing more than my copying a female cartoon character I had seen, and so it wasn't different from embroidering on an existing pattern. And there were huge differences between Sam-rae and a cartoon character, though this didn't stop me from trying over and over again.

You see, I considered Sam-rae to be a character living a sad, tear-soaked life and therefore different from the one in the cartoon. Sometimes, without thinking, I just got up and set off to town, but this kind of impulsive trip led nowhere since I would turn around mid-way.

I folded one of the drawings of her face and stashed it in my secret place in the wall. It was the niche in the wall where Sam-rae had hidden her treasures last winter. I saw it as a secret place that only she and I knew about. Harboring some obscure hope, I now and then peeked into the hole but didn't see any trace of Sam-rae having been there.

But one day in late December, as if taking Sam-rae's place, a woman in her early thirties with a baby on her back appeared. She said that she had missed the last bus in the village. Being in a difficult situation, she peeped into houses and eventually came to ours and asked us if she could thaw out her freezing body. Assuming a prim air, she had quite a fair face but looked exhausted from her long travel. It didn't seem, though, like she was seeking a meal under the pretext of warming herself up.

Sitting on the edge of our porch, tinged by the setting sun, she cleared her throat. Like a person who had just received her first paycheck, her throat clearing sounded somewhat exaggerated and I couldn't figure out why. Her outfit also puzzled me; she didn't at all dress like a woman on a long journey with a baby.

She wore red high heels and a Persian blue, two-piece suit that looked like too uncomfortable an outfit to wear on a long trip, especially with a suckling on her back. It was an outfit that gave the impression that she had the daring intention of transforming herself into an absolutely different person, one determined to forget everything about her baby once she was rid of it.

Soon she unburdened herself of the baby by placing it down on the porch's cold floor after untying the baby wrapper. But the baby, whose lips were pale and who slept soundly with his head leaning back, still didn't wake up, even after it rolled on the floor in its wrapper.

The baby soon woke up while its mother was in the outhouse. She took a long time in that rancid latrine with the smothering smell, and it seemed apparent to me that she was waiting for her baby to wake up and cry.

Meanwhile, half of the baby's lower body got uncovered and so it began crying with phlegm in its throat. Looking about a year or so old, the baby seemed to have a mild disposition; it cried but didn't make any frantic moves.

It was only when the baby burst out crying that my mother opened the door. Right then, the woman came out of the outhouse, shivering. Taking pity on the baby in the freezing weather outside, Mother asked the woman to come inside. But what the woman originally had asked for was just to sit on our porch for a short rest.

Pointing to the warm part of the room, Mother asked the woman, "Where are you going?"

"I'm going to Po-hang," she answered.

"What a hassle. And no buses are running now," Mother said.

"I heard there are inns in town," the woman responded.

"I see that you've begun a long trip in the middle of winter with a nursling on your back," Mother said.

Relaxing her body in the warm and cozy room, the woman now only nodded her head. Being considerate and aware that the woman wouldn't want to reveal what made her undertake such an arduous journey in the midst of a blizzard, Mother turned around towards the sewing machine and said, "Have a good rest and warm yourself up."

The baby kept crying, peevishly, and so its mother let it suck on a piece of dried fish that was tied to a string around the baby's neck. When the Mother put the piece into the baby's mouth, it stopped whining.

Right then, Mother, with her back to the woman, turned her head towards the baby and gave it a glance while still working at her sewing machine. It was common practice to give a just weaned baby a dried piece of sea mussel or abalone to calm it down, but it was a rare thing for my mother to see a dried pollack being used.

Lying down and looking about, the baby kept sucking on the dried fish. And its drowsy mother was now leaning against the wall and vacantly watching my mother sew. The woman didn't look like she was pressed for time. Sure enough, she soon fell into a deep sleep while her baby was sucking on the fish.

"She must've been very tired to just fall asleep like that," Mother said, quietly, while clicking her tongue, her way of revealing pity for others. I looked at the woman's white wrist that was propping up her head. The palm of her hand, which appeared as if she hadn't done any hard physical labor, was filled with clear but intricate lines, implying a troubled life. As if she had waited for the woman to fall asleep, Mother stopped sewing as soon as she did.

"Don't wake her up," Mother told me.

She then went into the kitchen wearing a somber face.

I was looking at the baby sucking on the dried fish, unaware that its mother was asleep. Its limbs, sticking out of the wrapper, were as lean as peeled cedar branches. Yes, it was obvious that the baby had a gentle disposition. And regardless of my unwelcoming glance, it kept nursing itself on the dried fish.

My eyes remained fixed on the baby's repetitive sucking motions. But I didn't see any of the fretting or voraciousness that a baby often shows when eating. Its sucking was the kind of habit that could've only been obtained through a mother's training over time.

Even for grown-ups dried mussel and abalone are so tough that they're not easily torn apart with teeth. But a dried pollack is different. It might take some time but when it's sucked in a mouth it becomes soft enough for even a just weaned baby to tear it with its new teeth. But since the baby was trained only to suck on it, the piece of fish more or less retained its shape and still hung on the string around the baby's neck.

The woman was now sleeping soundly and so I took a closer look at her face. Her eyes, nose, mouth, and ears were packed closely together on her small head, and it didn't look like she was struggling to eke out a livelihood. The woman slept with one hand on her forehead, as my mother used to do, and she looked peaceful, as if sleeping in her own home.

Right then, I heard Mother boil water in the cauldron in the kitchen. I knew that she was even going to prepare dinner for the uninvited visitor. But the sound Mother made while rinsing out the cauldron with a gourd before cooking rice in it wasn't the usual gentle one. She even dropped the gourd on the floor a couple of times.

I opened the door and stepped out onto the porch. Dusk had already covered the foot of the mountain. Black smoke billowed out of my neighbor's chimney and became white as it drifted quickly away towards the northern valley and dispersed in the wind. Nu-rung-jy, with his chin over the doorsill, looked up at me. Whenever the wind swirled against the door, the dog blinked his eyes.

The woman didn't wake up until dinner was almost ready. Awakened by the smell of steamed rice filling the room, she looked baffled. She glanced at the low table in the middle of the room with dishes on it, but her gaze finally stopped at my mother, who was still busy setting up the dinner table.

"I'm sorry. I must've fallen asleep. I should get my things together and leave," the woman said.

"Who could resist falling asleep after traveling such a long way in this bitter cold weather? Please join us, since it's already dinner time and you can leave after eating," Mother said.

"Oh, I didn't mean to inconvenience you like this."

Their conversation suddenly stopped and an awkward silence filled the air, but soon we started eating a meager meal, consisting of steamed mixed grains, watery soybean-paste soup, and stale old kimchi.

Contrary to my thinking that the woman, after her exhausting travels, would feed herself first, she first fed her baby very conscientiously. The woman chewed her first spoonful of rice then spit it out, little by little, to feed her baby with. She continued this until the baby pulled its head back from the food. She then began eating her meal. But she soon put her spoon down on the table after eating only several mouthfuls. It was then that my mother quickly picked up the woman's spoon and slipped it into her hand, saying, "Please, don't hold back and do help yourself. You don't think I'm going to charge you for your meal, do you? I'm not that kind of person."

Compliant, the woman took her spoon. But she looked as if she had no appetite and seemed to be going through the motions of eating. And this must've rubbed my mother the wrong way, since she didn't offer her anything more.

That night it snowed again and this gave the woman a good excuse to spend more time in our cottage to rest from her tiring travel.

Mother poured rice chaff into the burning kiln to heat up the room's floor, and its somewhat fishy smell seeped into the air. The two women, like hens sitting together on their eggs, soon began working together on a patchwork wrapper.

Not long afterwards, I fell asleep, but now and then I woke up and heard their whisperings hovering in the air, whisperings light as dust, free of any agitation or confrontation. They didn't have anything in common, but there wasn't any tension in their dialogue at all. The baby slept through the night and woke up early the following morning. Hearing her baby's whimpering the woman immediately woke up and said in a dry voice, "He has to pee this time in the morning."

It sounded to me like she was speaking to my mother. I heard bustling sounds as the woman lifted up the comforter and opened and shut the door. After peeing in a pot on the porch, the baby went back to sleep, like a baby doll, and the two women began their day. I heard the woman's concerned voice.

"We had a lot of snow last night."

It was right then that Mother said, "Se-young, we need to clear the snow, at least in front of the kitchen."

Getting up, I went out and grabbed a wooden shovel, and

soon the woman also appeared in the yard. Her face was neat and clean, without any trace of last night's fatigue. For a moment she gazed at the distant snow-covered hills and mountains, but soon turned around and told me, "Would you pass me the shovel? I'd like to help."

Holding out her white hands, she tried to take the shovel from me. Her warm palms covered my hands. Suddenly, I missed Sam-rae. And I wished the woman's soft warm hands were hers.

Where was Sam-rae during last night's snowfall? Where would such a woman have spent a cold snowy night, a woman who's not afraid of any change that life has to offer?

"Your name must be Se-young," asked the woman.

Without saying a word, I nodded while looking the other way.

"And you're fourteen years old, right?" she asked.

I didn't like anyone asking my age. To me being fourteen, like the number of cement steps in an abandoned building, was something that made me feel that I was insignificant and was being watched by someone as well. But it seemed that Mother had told her such a trivial thing as my age.

And I knew that to the woman, who was traveling to wherever, something like my age wasn't really important. So I just ignored her question and tried to stop Nu-rung-jy's barking after he spotted a stranger with me and ran up to us.

Receiving my cold response, the woman was quick to close her mouth. For a while she seemed engrossed with clearing the snow away in front of the kitchen. While doing so, steam rose from the nape of her neck. It was then that I was reprimanded by my mother.

"Se-young, it's your job, not hers!"

The woman handed the shovel back to me while wiping away the sweat from her forehead in a somewhat exaggerated manner. The baby didn't wake up until we were eating breakfast. I was almost wondering if he had been drugged with a sleeping pill. I also wondered whether his mental development was impaired or not. But when the woman woke the baby up, he immediately and without any whining opened his shiny eyes, which didn't look like they were just jerked out of a deep sleep, and began eating the food spooned into his mouth. My mother admired this.

"What a baby! He isn't even shy of strangers," Mother exclaimed.

"Well, I didn't expect it, either. He's usually fussy and doesn't act like this," the woman replied.

"Yes, he looks like he has a small appetite, but thankfully, he eats this meager meal," my mother said.

"Maybe he knows that we're not home, even though he can't speak," said the woman.

"Anyway, this village is encircled by hills, and when we have a big snowfall like this, it's common that all transportation is cut off for days," said Mother.

"Yes, that concerned me, too," said the woman.

"It's a long way to Po-hang. Please make this your home and you can leave when the snow melts," Mother said to her.

"Thank you for your kindness, but I'm not in a situation where I can put off leaving," the woman said.

"But how can you leave when the road is blocked like this?" Mother asked.

"Well, do you think I can catch a bus to Po-hang if I go to town?" she asked.

"But it snowed in town, too. And even though there's a bus, the road wouldn't be safe to travel," said Mother.

It wasn't easy for me to understand why Mother was trying to postpone her leaving. There was no reason that I knew of for Mother, who hadn't even hung out with the village women when she easily could've, to insist on having a stranger stay with us. And my mother wasn't the kind of woman who said things to be polite and only later regrets it.

What perplexed me more was that the woman was determined to leave regardless of my mother's urging her not to. She was different from Sam-rae, who withstood beatings and humiliation in order to remain with us last winter. Yes, I had misjudged the woman from the beginning.

Complying with my mother's earnest appeal, the woman unwillingly stayed one more night, fretting all the while. But the following morning she left for town shortly after finishing her breakfast, saying that she had to find out if there was some kind of transportation to where she was going and that she'd return shortly. It would take about one hour for her to walk to town and back, and meanwhile, Mother was in charge of taking care of the baby while the woman was gone. But the woman didn't return even after hours had passed.

For the first time, I waited for a strange woman from morning till evening. When the sun was about to set I began walking to and fro between our house and the main road to the village, waiting for the woman. But it was all in vain.

It was after the sun had set and a lamp was lit in our room that I found my mother. Since the woman had left in the morning, Mother didn't leave her room. Buried in her sewing jobs that she had gotten before the snowfall, she worked throughout the day. Oh yes, when I said *I found* my mother, I didn't mean that she had disappeared but rather that I found something new in her that evening.

I then realized that Mother hadn't said a word the whole day. Furthermore, she didn't even open the door or get on the road to see whether the woman was returning or not. When I went back and forth to the main road, Mother also seemed to be ignoring my fretting. The only thing she did was to ask me to thread the sewing machine needle.

The last two nights Mother had even put away her sewing

orders and hadn't gotten enough sleep in order to have more time to talk with the woman, but after she had disappeared like smoke, regardless of her promise to return within an hour, Mother spent the whole day apparently without any concern.

Meanwhile, the baby woke up several times. And whenever this happened, Mother slipped the dried fish into its mouth to prevent it from crying, a cry that was ready to burst out at any time. At sunset Mother even made some rice gruel for the baby, and it ate every spoonful without fretting.

I lit the lamp and sat in the room and watched Mother's hunched back as she worked at her sewing machine. At times, when the sounds of the machine stopped, the snowstorm, whipped up by the winter's north wind, struck the door.

A long silence had settled into the darkness, a darkness that had descended to the foot of the mountains. Suddenly, I missed Sam-rae. Tears filled my eyes. And I felt my fatigue had contracted my heart and now weighed on my shoulders. Shortly, I heard the rustling sounds of clothes.

"You must be tired. Go to bed," Mother said.

In her soft voice I felt that she was trying to soothe her own disturbed mind. With my chin, I motioned to the baby who was sleeping in the warm side of the room and asked Mother, "When is she coming back?"

"She's not coming back," Mother said.

It felt somehow odd and unexpected that she said so in such a confident manner, but, nonetheless, I asked her the same question again.

"If not today then when is she coming back?"

"Well, maybe in five or ten years. But probably she won't ever return," said Mother.

"What are you talking about? She's the mother of this baby. It doesn't make sense to me at all that she isn't coming back.

Maybe she'll come back tomorrow after spending a night in town because the road was blocked by snow," I said.

"Listen, if she could get to town she should also be able to return. I know she won't be back. From the very beginning she came here with the intention of dropping off her baby, so there's no reason for her to come back," said Mother.

I was upset with what she said and sullenly asked her, "Why our home out of all the others?"

"No one would drop off their baby and run away for no reason. There's a good explanation for this," said Mother.

She then looked up at the ceiling and continued talking to herself.

"How meaningful it is, having this big snowfall. It's been mainly during winter that difficult things have happened to me and also have been solved. I married your father on a snowy winter day like today."

But she didn't mention that father had also left us on a winter day. Maybe it was abominable to even utter that he had abandoned her. Her pale lips shivered. She again looked up at the ceiling, but in the end her pathetic eyes shed tears.

"Before my marriage, my older brother was critical of your father. Now I know that a man has maybe a more perceptive eye than a woman when it comes to judging a man. My brother insisted on my postponing the marriage until the following spring, but I disregarded his advice and hurriedly married your father on a cold winter day in my parents' yard after clearing the snow. It was my fault; I was a straight arrow and inexperienced with the ways of the world and made a mistake and gave in to your father's fervent appeals. I then gave my straightforward account to my parents of what had happened between your father and me, and this hastened my marriage, but I didn't know then that it would cause a fallout between my brother and us," Mother said.

"Tomorrow I'll go to town and look for her," I told Mother.

"It's no use. And you don't do such a useless thing in this kind of weather, anyway. Do you think the woman hasn't come back because she got lost?" said Mother.

I was so upset with Mother's attitude, especially when she even discouraged my wanting to search for the woman, that I stood as if I was about to give the baby a hard kick. It was right at that moment that I heard Mother's matter of fact statement, "This baby is your brother."

They were the exact words that had been hovering in my mind. Even before Mother had said that no woman existed who would just drop off her own baby and run away without any reason, I had this very suspicion, one that had been obsessing me. But I had waited for either my mother or the woman to clear up the baby's true identity.

Turning her eyes away from me, Mother approached the baby in its wrapper and lifted it up to her bosom. When it opened its eyes, Mother slipped the dried fish into its mouth. And she then talked to it, as if talking to herself.

"Eat something, you little thing, don't just suck."

As if Mother's strange voice wasn't soothing to the baby, who had just awoken from its sleep, it first stuck out its lips and looked like it was about to cry but soon began sucking on the dried fish. Mother again talked to herself.

"I knew from the beginning that all this was caused by your father."

We found a small pouch that was wrapped around the baby's waist and in it found the baby's name, Ho-young, and its birthday, and also some money. They were the things that the woman had left with her baby.

Even though Mother had decided to accept the baby without any complaint, the reality that she was now facing could turn out to be shameful and humiliating. But there was also a chance, I thought, that she took it as a sign that my father would return to her soon and not as sign of some kind of betrayal or humiliation.

Maybe Mother's waiting would end soon, I thought. But there wasn't any way for me and my mother, a woman making a meager living while hiding from the world, to conceal what was happening to us. No possibility existed to declare the baby as being my younger brother without stirring up gossip and rumors. It was a huge challenge for my mother, who hadn't acknowledged any rumor except for the one that said my father had left her.

After spending that night with the baby, Mother seemed to have grasped what was involved in her situation. What frightened her the most was the baby's crying. She hadn't expected the baby's bold and frantic crying once it realized that it was no longer held by familiar hands.

And the enormous shits that accompanied its crying turned out to be a nightmare at our house, a house already bleak enough. It cried, too, when it was either held or put down.

The late night silence of the mountain village, where the day's footsteps and shadows had already evaporated, was so deep that one could even recall memories from the forgotten past, and in this dead silence, the baby's cries throughout that night sounded like the wailings of a ghost.

The baby's cries exhausted my mother. Worn out, it fell asleep in the early morning. But even this sleep made us more depressed; it seemed that it was sleeping only to prepare itself for the coming night's crying and defecating.

That night the whole house became a mess and Mother realized that she wouldn't be able to just brush away what was happening. And I saw on her gloomy face that there wasn't anything we could do about it. What she did best that night was just fondle the baby's buttocks.

"Se-young, what can we do? We can't plug up its mouth every

night, can we?" Mother asked me. She said this the morning after we had spent that first night with the baby. But just like Mother, I also had no idea how to stop the baby's wailing. Well, as a matter of fact, I had a way, even though it was extreme: To abandon it at a lonely place in the snow. And then I spit out words that only a desperate person would say: "If you plug up its mouth, it'll smother to death."

"Don't say such a terrible thing, even in a dream . . . you'll get punished by Heaven. How, as a human being, can you say such a horrible thing?" Mother said.

"Then how can you stop the crying every night?" I asked her.

"Never mind the crying . . . even though it makes an ox's sounds, how could you utter such a thing as plugging up a baby's mouth?" said Mother.

"Well, wasn't it you who said it first?" I retorted.

"Did I?" Mother said.

"Did you forget what you've just said?" I told her.

I saw Mother's pale lips quivering. She then began coughing. Grasping the doorsill, she tried to calm her coughing by holding her breath, but this made her thin shoulders shudder as if she was sobbing; I quickly turned my eyes away from her.

Barely managing to stop coughing, she opened the door. It was a fine sunny day, but the only thing I could see outside was frozen snow everywhere. The orange-colored sunlight was reflecting on the snow-covered roofs that slanted down northwards. Dazzled by the dense light's reflection, Mother shielded her eyes. The fresh winter wind rushed into the room and I felt like it was inflating my body like a balloon, giving me a very pleasant sensation, a sensation that I liked more than the one I experienced when I was in the warm part of the room. Mother's gaze was fixed above the snow, where the snow-covered field met the sky.

"What do we do with this baby?" she muttered, in a voice choked with sorrow.

"Maybe I'll go to Mr. Jang and talk to him," I told her.

I expected Mother to be startled at my suggestion. It was him whom Mother had feared the most before the baby arrived. But contrary to what I had expected, she didn't react. I left the room and stepped on the porch, but she still didn't respond.

Sensing Mother's desperate gaze behind me, I began running. And when I was far enough away from home, far enough so that any change in Mother wouldn't stop me from doing what I decided on, I finally stopped and caught my breath.

Jang was in his rice mill. Since Nu-rung-jy had already run over to him and informed him of my arrival, he was outside the mill where the sunlight was warm. With his arms crossed, he seemed to have already read my mind.

"You're here because of the woman who came to your house with a baby, right?"

"Yes."

"And she left her baby behind and disappeared, right?"

"Yes," I repeated.

"What a predicament," he said.

The word "predicament" pricked my heart painfully, like an awl. And what was strange was that he knew about everything that had happened in our house as though he was watching us in a mirror, regardless of the fact that my mother lived a reclusive life away from any social contact. It was as if he lived under the floor of our cottage.

He lit his cigarette and held it in his mouth. While blowing out smoke, he looked somewhat lighthearted and satisfied.

"And of course, there isn't any way to find out where she's living. Listen, when you search for a person you should follow the Five-Ws and One-H Principle: who, what, when, where, why, and how. But even though your mother is a woman of keen sensibility and common sense, she still wouldn't know such a thing. Finding the woman would be like plucking a star from the sky with a stick. And since I've never met her, my knowing the Five-Ws and One-H Principle won't help, either," Jang said.

"So you're saying it's impossible to find the baby's mother?" I asked.

"Didn't you understand what I just said? It's like plucking a star from the sky, got it? Your mother let the woman leave, and it wasn't just a whim of hers to let it happen, so she's not going to try and find her."

Putting out his cigarette on the doorpost, he squatted down and leaned against the mud-plastered wall. Sunlight was shining across a corner of his shirt that was covered with white dust.

"I know that your mother is a stubborn lady, you see. I just don't understand why she can't relate heart-to-heart with me. Why do you think we have this old saying: A good neighbor is better than a distant cousin? That's because sometimes neighbors need to be more openhearted about things and find solutions when they're having difficulties, and that's another form of exchanging labor. Your mother, though, is proud and a straight arrow, see, and that's her problem. But since I know what's happening, don't worry and go back home. Even though I dislike your mother's ways, as a neighbor I won't turn my back on her," said Jang.

He seemed to take offense at the way my mother was handling her situation. Taking out the cigarette that he had just put out, he again held it between his lips. I knew they must've talked about the situation and didn't know what kind of talk they had, but when he said "don't worry and go back home," I had the impression that he had some way to solve the problem.

With my hands in my pockets, I turned around. Deep inside my pocket I found a roasted bean. And just like the bean that came out of the blue, I wished Sam-rae was within my reach.

When I came back home, Ho-young was sleeping and Mother was

working at her sewing machine. She seemed to have somewhat regained her composure. When I opened the door, though, she didn't even turn around but remained with her back to me. I knew that she didn't want to reveal her distress. Bluntly, I told Mother, "He said don't worry."

Mother, though, didn't say anything. I understood her struggle to maintain her pride and dignity as a woman. But all that was just a snare that she had created all by herself and placed around her own neck.

Maybe it was just my bungling conclusion, though. There was something that made me suspect some kind of secret link existed between Jang and my mother, since he knew exactly what was on her mind.

But even though they had their secret door to each other that only they could use, it no longer piqued my curiosity like before. Rather, during those times my head was filled with Sam-rae and the baby, who brought me enough distress, leaving me little room to watch over Mother. But it was obvious that the baby brought about a huge change in her.

With the baby, Mother was now short of hands, and so she decided to find a helper from among the village women, someone she knew. But it took days for her to find the right person; from the beginning she had hesitated in deciding whether or not to get a helper, until at last she decided on a woman called Chang-beom's mother.

On the first day the helper came to our house, she said to Mother, "I heard that the baby's mother is your distant relative from your home village. And I heard that she had died right after its birth. It would've been difficult for the baby to survive if it hadn't met a person like you doing such a benevolent deed. How kind of you in this harsh and coldhearted world." The woman didn't hold back in complimenting my mother in such an extravagant manner, obviously wanting the job as Mother's sewing assistant. This remark of hers immediately released Mother from her concerns relating to the baby.

After listening to her, Mother finally hired the lady as her helper. I then realized what Jang meant when he said don't worry about the baby and go back home.

And with the lady working as Mother's sewing assistant, Mother finally began to gradually step out into the world.

3

One market day, after about two weeks had passed since the woman dropped off Ho-young, Mother and I went to town together. Only after we arrived at the marketplace did I find out that we were there to buy a rooster.

It was early morning when we arrived, and waiting for people with chickens to sell while standing against a sunny mud wall was boring. It looked like we needed to wait a long time before the chicken market was fully ready to open. This was because of Mother, who had hurried so early in the morning to get there. If I remember correctly, we'd never before raised chickens. And, furthermore, I knew that Mother didn't have enough spare time to feed chickens or take care of a chicken coop.

As soon as the market was open, Mother intently searched for a rooster with splendid feathers. Combing the market place thoroughly, she searched everywhere in order to find the rooster that she had envisioned in her mind.

But it wasn't easy to find Mother's ideal rooster. Even though it turned out that finding a native rooster with plump dark-red cockscombs on the crown of its head, feathers perfectly balanced between dark red and a dazzling black, and a rakish tail shooting upwards, was unlikely, Mother didn't easily give up.

After, we went into a rice-cake store at one corner of the market to catch our breath and have some rice-cakes to soothe our empty stomachs. It was close to noon. By then we were both exhausted from the cold weather.

But, like Mother, I also didn't want to give up trying to find the ideal rooster. And even though I couldn't fathom what was on her mind, I was happy to see her for the first time deeply involved in something other than sewing, and besides, I also actually kind of liked searching for a handsome native rooster.

Disregarding winter's short daylight, we still waited for the rooster to appear and be chosen by us. Finally, our patience and labor bore fruit—we at last noticed an old woman holding a rooster in her bosom, the kind that we had been looking for. Mother's face, which had looked cheerless because of her disappointment and the cold weather, immediately beamed brightly.

Soon the haggling began, but Mother didn't beat down the price. She paid the amount the old woman wanted and almost snatched the warm rooster from her. Buying hens was now the next thing for us to do. Mother, without bargaining, soon bought two babbling hens that appeared to be laying eggs the moment they arrived at our cottage.

At home Mother tied the chickens to a pole on the porch to tame them, and once they became familiar with their new place after three days, I finally learned why she bought them. It happened the day when one of the two hens laid the first egg and Mother picked it up in the yard, her face beaming with delight. All that day, the hens had hung out with the rooster.

"At least it seems that I've chosen the right chickens," Mother exclaimed.

Like the babbling hens, Mother also talked to herself when picking up the eggs and tenderly petting them. Until then I didn't know whether Mother had bought the chickens for meat, hatching chicks, or for eggs.

But one day I took a trip to town and an unexpected event blotted out all my thoughts of either chickens or eggs. I went to the tavern where Sam-rae had once worked for a short period.

Ever since Ho-young had come to our home, I'd been very much engaged in trying to adjust myself to a new environment and had at times forgotten about Sam-rae. But that day I missed her so much. Her face was everywhere; even fallen leaves burning in the kitchen's kiln had Sam-rae's face on them.

It was several days after we had brought home the chickens from the market that I visited the tavern at sunset. Repeating the words "have guts" to myself, I stood in the middle of the tavern's yard and called out for the owner.

When the bar owner opened the door, I became conscious of my short height, so I lifted up my heels in order to look more like a grown man. Splendid lights rushed out from inside and spread across the yard. With her head bent slantwise, she asked me, "Do I know you? Would you come closer to me?"

What am I doing here? I was embarrassed and ashamed of myself. But I knew that it was too late to turn back. Thinking that I needed to look manly and imposing, I walked towards the porch where a white porcelain chamber pot was located. But soon the owner noticed that I was a stranger to her. Looking shapely and well-mannered, the woman then gave me a disagreeable look, saying, "Well, I don't think I know you. What do you want?"

Thinking that I needed to quickly get control of an awkward situation, I said, without reserve,

"I'm here to get Sam-rae's address. She worked here not long ago."

For a moment the woman seemed to balk at my request, but then shouted at someone inside the room, "Min, do you know who Sam-rae is?"

A welcomed answer immediately came out of the room.

"Sam-rae? Isn't that Mi-sook's real name?"

"Well, then, where's Mi-sook now?" the owner asked.

"She must be in Dae-goo."

"Where in Dae-goo?"

"Let me get the address."

The woman named Min glanced at me and then rummaged through her dressing table's drawers. She soon jotted something down with her eyebrow pencil and handed the paper to me.

Carefully folding it, I put it in my pocket and left. A cold gust of wind grazed the walls in the alleyway. I felt a sudden dizziness as I hurried to get out of the alley and so I stood against the wall. When my giddiness eased up, I took a matchbox out of my pocket. I lit five or six matches, but the beautiful poppy blossom didn't appear before me.

To me, Dae-goo was a city that was as far away as a cliff at the end of the world. At that time the Himalayas were closer to me. When I heard the name of the city, Dae-goo, from the woman inside the tavern, I still didn't have much hope of seeing Sam-rae again. But on the way back home, I repeated the name "Dae-goo" endlessly to myself.

It was that night I saw why Mother had bought the chickens.

In an attempt to avoid her scolding me for coming home late, I muffled my footsteps while crossing the yard. The room was lit but silent. Mother and Ho-young were probably sleeping, I thought. Uncomfortable in darkness, Mother used to sleep with her lamplight on.

Quietly, I opened the door. I saw Mother, with her back to me, in the middle of the room, crouching down like potted chrysanthemum flowers. But she was so engrossed in something that she seemed to have lost her usual keen sense of presence.

Only after I entered the room did Mother, who was holding and breastfeeding Ho-young in her bosom, turn around, startled. I saw her plump breasts beneath her rolled-up *jeo-go-ri*. Unexpectedly witnessing this scene, I, without thinking, let out a scream. Forcefully, I flung open the door and left the room and stepped out on the cold porch, slamming the door behind me. From the room I heard the rustling sounds that Mother made as she adjusted her *jeo-go-ri* and the sounds of the hatch door to the kitchen opening and shutting. Mother seemed to be concerned with my harsh emotional reaction.

What had happened right before I had returned home was that Ho-young was whimpering after waking up from his nap, so Mother broke an egg and fed him the yolk. But the baby didn't stop crying.

Agitated, Mother naturally opened her *jeo-go-ri* and had the baby suck on her breast. As soon as he began sucking, the baby stopped crying. Mother was completely captivated by the magic of it all. The reason I was so upset was because it dawned on me that Mother hadn't raised me with such affection.

It wasn't easy to understand her that night. Seeing her maternal love showered on Ho-young and not me brought despair and frustration.

Her love for Ho-young meant nothing to me. And by acting like that, Mother succeeded in hurting me without even using a rod.

My heart was smarting. And Mother's love became a threat, more than violence or hatred. But above all the most hurtful thing, besides her forcing Sam-rae to leave me, was her committing such a betrayal.

I missed Sam-rae, who was passionate but tranquil, intense but collected, sad but exciting, missed everything about her, my heart overflowing like a waterfall gushing over a cliff. I heard Mother's subdued voice asking me to see if everything was okay in the chicken coop before coming back inside. I did what I was told and was about to go to my room when Mother said, "Will you sit down? We need to talk."

I stood there, looking around at where I had lived for fourteen years, but for some reason, I couldn't find a spot to sit down that felt like home. I felt awkward and uncomfortable, as if I was in a strange place. Though it was a small space, I, nonetheless, suddenly became confused about how much distance I should put between Mother and me. Right then, she said, sarcastically, "The ceiling won't collapse, even though you don't prop it up. So sit down there. Where have you been?"

"Just hanging out," I answered.

"You know you should be studying, not hanging out."

"Yes, I know."

"How brazen you are, answering me like that," Mother said.

"Yes," I answered again.

"Did you just say "yes" to me again?"

"Yes, I did."

"Are you doing this on purpose to upset me . . . answering like that?"

"No, I'm not," I said.

"Whatever you say, I know what you've been up to," said Mother.

She probably knew that my lame answers would only make her more suspicious and worsen the situation, for she suddenly stopped her inquisition. That night both Mother and I hid our sense of shame while throwing barbed words at each other and avoiding the conflict between us.

We were no longer a mother and a son who read each other's minds and who were very attentive to each other's needs. The village stream that had frozen up at the beginning of that winter and the heavy silence hovering over the village swamp seemed to symbolize the antagonism between Mother and me.

Racked by loneliness and emptiness and a sense of being betrayed, all of it accumulating in my heart, layer after layer, I began roaming aimlessly along the desolate embankments, where only wilted grassroots were scattered about. I finally came to believe that, just like my father, I had to leave home, too.

Every morning, though, I continued as usual to sweep the yard, feed the chickens, and have breakfast before hurriedly leaving home like I had something urgent to do. Afterwards, I would cross farmland before hiking up the village hill and taking a close look at the icy stream and swamp below.

The stream, where the previous summer young men had dissolved wild pepper juice into the water in order to kill and then scoop up gourdfuls of plump carps, was now shallow and filled with jagged pieces of ice.

And the hill, where red dragonflies, red as well-ripened peppers, had flown about during summer and autumn, now became the setting for restless gusts of wind blowing from every direction, but I couldn't see my father anywhere. And on the back side of fallen tree barks, all tumbling around on the ground, hibernating ladybugs were swarming about.

Now and then I stopped and gave an icy glare at my house. But every time I did so, tears filled my eyes and trickled down my cheeks and I couldn't see anything. I could no longer see my mother, who, like a clear mirror, had always helped me on my way whenever things became murky.

Mother's devotion to Ho-young even bewildered Chang-beom's mother. Like a monk who devotedly meditates in order to attain illumination, Mother seemed determined to dedicate her heart and all her energy to the baby.

Feeding the chickens was my job, but Mother always collected the eggs for Ho-young. And when he didn't show any interest in eating fresh yolk, Mother would then mix it with honey and spoon-feed the delicacy to him. Like a new mother, she mostly stayed in the warm part of the room with the baby resting on her bosom and let Chang-beom's mother do the sewing.

I even wondered whether Mother was having Ho-young

revert back to his nursling stage, a baby already weaned from its mother's breast. Her devotion to him made me believe that she would regret not having had more to give, even after giving everything to him, and this obsessive affection upset even her helper, who advised her that she'd spoil the child if she continued what she was doing, but Mother ignored her. Mother also didn't show any concern about what I was going through—confusion and alienation.

It was about that time that I began to hang out at Jang's rice mill. It was okay for anyone to visit and so I went there often. It was the perfect place to increase my hatred for my mother.

Above all, I began to enjoy standing against the mill's adobe wall that was connected to railings and pillars and that shivered and shuddered as if it would collapse at any time once the machines began roaring. Actually, there was a hole in the wall where a railing and a pillar met, big enough for a fist to travel through. And when the machines started rumbling, it seemed the wall would crack at any moment. But, nonetheless, even without any repairs the mud wall kept standing.

I stood there with my back glued to the wall, and when it began shaking, shaking not only my body but also my intestines, the adrenaline in me would surge. These jolting movements pierced through my skin and reached my bones and shook my joints, somehow confirming that I too, like countless others, possessed an evil power that could hate and tear into anyone. And my sadness and sense of betrayal churned inside me, along with the wall's rumbling. And by then, my accumulated hatred for Mother, along with my racing heart, would gain momentum and I would imagine giving in to an urge for action.

It was a place that constantly reminded me of why I was shivering in the cold like a dog and why I had to hate my mother. It helped nourish my hatred and offered me some excitement and freedom from her.

I sometimes peeped into the mill, too. In the midst of the noise coming from the old machines and belts, I saw Jang and his workers, all covered with white dust from rice and wheat bran, walking around inside. With their winter caps covering their earlobes and thick masks concealing their noses and with their sluggish movements and their dust-covered whiskers and eyebrows, they reminded me of grizzly bears in the tundra.

Jang and the workers would effortlessly lift up heavy straw bags of grain and shift them around, farting all the while. Such simple labor also reminded me of the movements of dull-witted bears. I would wait for the day to end while absent-mindedly watching the sauntering bears imitate human beings inside the mill.

Jang didn't give me a strange look, even after discovering that I was loitering at his mill, nor did he ever ask me what I was doing there. Because of this, I could closely observe his daily routine, something I hadn't paid attention to before. And just like his work, his daily routine was also simple and boring.

One day at sunset, when all the machines stopped at the same time, the place suddenly fell into a deep silence. As I followed the grizzly bear Jang, who left the mill first, a winter dusk fell across the field.

On his way this grizzly bear met with villagers who greeted him, but he simply nodded his head to them. He then, instead of taking the main road, took a shortcut across rice fields.

Arriving at his cottage, which looked cold and unhomely, even from the exterior, he first glanced at ours before entering his yard. Once there, he didn't go directly into his room but went into the kitchen and bolted the door and took off his thick winter jacket.

Soon he heated up some water in a big cauldron and filled his tub with it. The kitchen by then was filled with steam billowing from the tub, making it hard to see anything clearly.

He walked to the tub, and as he slowly immersed his nude body in the hot water up to his neck, the water overflowed and spilled onto the kitchen's dirt floor. Once his body was submerged, he gazed up at the ceiling. He then finally opened his mouth, firmly sealed since he left the mill, and said, "Ah . . . this is so good."

He soon began shaking his hands in the water as if searching for something.

I became uneasy, expecting to see a big fat salmon struggling to escape and at any moment being snagged out of the water by him.

If there weren't any salmon there, which I read somewhere struggles to swim up stream against the current during its spawning season, his arms wouldn't have had to move that intensely in the water. Or he may've been rubbing dead skin away from his groin or armpits.

And if that wasn't the case, then he may've been checking his paws to see if they were functioning properly, thinking that they might've atrophied while he hadn't used them. But no, that couldn't have been the case. His movements, which looked as if he was floundering in a fog, reminded me of a bear's awkward dance in swirling water while searching for fish.

He didn't, though, catch a salmon in the tub as I had expected, but instead, he kept farting, creating bursting bubbles in the water. He soon suddenly pulled his body out of the tub, as if he himself were a salmon soaring against the stream's currents.

Something happened one day that greatly affected my mother. Our rooster didn't come home, even after dusk. I checked the rack inside the chicken coop three times but only saw our two hens hunched over at one corner and didn't see the cock that Mother cherished the most next to Ho-young. Anxiously, she and I waited for it until it became dark, but it still didn't show up, and there were no signs of it anywhere. The rooster had never before made us worry like that.

Finally, Mother laid Ho-young down in the room and sat on the porch. She looked wretched, like some ghost. Since it became dark, the temperature suddenly dropped, and fallen oak leaves, wet with snow, were rolling about gloomily on the ground. I was standing in the front yard when Mother asked me, aggressively and in a stinging tone, about our rooster's whereabouts.

"It doesn't make any sense to me that you don't know where it is. You should know where it hangs out, since you too leave home as soon as you finish your meal and stay out all day, just like the rooster," said Mother.

"What makes you think I would know where it is when I didn't follow it around all day?" I retorted.

"You don't have to follow it all the time to know where it goes. Don't you have any idea which manure heap it usually hangs out at? Being a simple creature, it may've entered some other house's chicken coop. And how could you know nothing about it?" Mother said, with needles in her words.

"The rooster isn't that dumb. It's never before entered another house's coop," I answered.

"But who knows, if some hen approached it and coo-cooed it, being dumb and simple enough, it would follow it, wouldn't it?" asked Mother.

"We have two hens home, so I don't think it would've followed any neighbor's hen," I said.

"Stop talking nonsense. And what do you know about what attracts hens or roosters, anyway?" said Mother, snidely.

"I'm just answering your question, Mother," I said.

"As the saying goes, birds of a feather flock together, so are you siding with your kind?"

"I don't know what you're talking about," I snapped.

"Why don't you stop wasting time talking back to your

mother? Go search our neighbors' coops for our rooster!" ordered Mother.

"It'll come home, if we wait a little longer," I responded.

"You had better stop talking back," Mother said.

She then, in a somewhat dejected voice, called on Chang-beom's mother who was working at the sewing machine. Having been ordered to go search for the chicken, I walked through the gate while repeatedly thinking to myself, *I should leave. I've gotta leave here.*

I methodically checked all my neighbors' chicken coops, but our rooster was nowhere to be seen. It seemed to have disappeared like smoke. My stomach was growling with hunger when I began my search, but after not finding the rooster, it seemed to be growling even louder, and this made me feel cross and miserable. I thought that I should return home and argue with Mother more to release my frustration and anger.

On the way back home from the rooster search that night, I happened to see my mother at a totally unexpected place. When I was entering through our gate, I spotted two women in front of Jang's kitchen door.

It was dark and at first I thought they were strangers. But approaching closer, I clearly saw who they were: my mother and Chang-beom's mother. I was so surprised to see them there that I stopped suddenly, as if my head had struck a wall.

Clinging to the door, the two women were totally engrossed in watching something through a small opening. And what astonished me the most was my mother. I was shocked because she rarely visited any of our neighbors unless it was absolutely necessary. That night, though, she, of her own free will, was at the home of the man whom she had seemingly shunned more than anyone else in the whole village. It must've been Chang-beom's mother who first saw Jang taking a bath in his kitchen, but still, she wouldn't have forced my mother to join her. Like ghosts in white dress trying to sneak into Jang's kitchen, the two women gripped the door and didn't look like they would leave anytime soon.

Muffling my footsteps, I quickly returned home. Ho-young was alone resting in the warm part of the room. Even though he was by himself, he didn't cry, but rather was babbling while looking up at the ceiling. I lifted him up and put him on my lap. With his weight on my thighs, baby odors rushed into my nostrils. I realized then that it was my first time holding him.

I looked down at the baby gazing up at me. His facial features were more distinctive than when he had first appeared. I rolled up my fist and mimicked striking his nose with it. It was something I wanted to do if the opportunity ever came someday.

Contrary to my expectation, he didn't burst out crying but rather almost smiled. It was then that I heard footsteps coming from the yard and so I hurriedly put the baby down. I heard Mother talking to herself as she took off her shoes before stepping on the porch: "What a shameful thing to do . . . for sure a sane man in his right mind wouldn't do that."

But Chang-beom's mother immediately replied to Mother's soliloquy: "It's been a long time since I saw something like that, so it was rather fun to watch."

Getting into the room, Chang-beom's mother giggled while covering her mouth with her sleeve. Mother gave her a sharp look. Maybe it was due to the cold weather, but I noticed that Mother's cheeks were glowing red.

Mother seemed to be startled at seeing me sitting in the room. But she soon recovered her calm and inquired about the rooster.

"Did you find that bastard?"

"No, I didn't. I don't think we'll find it tonight, especially since I have no idea where that bastard went."

Right then, Mother scolded me in a high-pitched voice, "That bastard! A young boy shouldn't speak that way."

"What should I call it if I shouldn't call it that? Maybe I'll call it uncle," I retorted.

"Are you talking back to your mother again?" she fumed.

Right then, I realized that I shouldn't have talked that way to my mother. Because of my behavior, I sensed her sadness settling deep inside her. I stood up.

"I'll look for it one more time," I said.

"I'll go with you," Mother responded.

After having watched us, Chang-beom's mother tried to dissuade us from going, saying, "This mother and son must've decided to freeze to death tonight. It's close to midnight, you know."

But Mother put her silk scarf around her neck and told me, "Never mind midnight, we have to go and find it, even if it were daybreak. The rooster is a part of our family, even though it's a mere animal that can't speak."

"Well, aren't you in the end going to butcher it for food? Why do you fuss over a chicken this cold night? It'll probably come back tomorrow morning after spending the night in one of the neighbors' chicken coops," Chang-beom's mother said.

Hearing this, Mother stopped straightening her clothes for a moment and glared at her helper, her eyes brimming with hostility. But Mother didn't argue any longer. As we left the cottage, my heart began pounding, since I already knew what had happened to the chicken. And it was something that I would never tell Mother about under any circumstances.

That was how our pilgrimage to the village that night began. What surprised me, though, was that Mother, who had rarely visited any neighbors before, knew exactly which houses were raising chickens. She pointed them out to me and told me to take a look.

That night's search for the rooster in our neighbors' chicken coops could've resulted in our getting lambasted by the villagers if we were caught. Yes, if by any chance our trespassing on other people's property was spotted by anyone, Mother would've done irreparable damage to her reputation as a woman living without a husband. But it seemed this didn't bother her that much.

And so that night we became trespassers. When I sneaked into a yard and peeped into the chicken coop for our rooster, Mother, leaning against a wall, stood guard near the gate of the cottage. I thought it was ironic that the people who lived there and who needed to guard their property were sleeping soundly in their rooms while my mother, an intruder, was guarding instead. But she, usually of keen common sense, didn't seem to realize this.

Anyway, I gradually got to enjoy being a trespasser in the bitter cold. What thrilled me was rummaging through people's backyards and chicken coops accompanied by a guard while the world was asleep. And the rare opportunity to witness Mother's misjudgment and ultimate failure in finding the chicken also delighted me.

We searched chicken coops even though they weren't exactly in our neighborhood, but it was all in vain. Mother, though, still hadn't given up yet. Her eagerness and anxiousness was such a hilarious thing to watch; I enjoyed it as if relishing roasted sunflower seeds, since I knew that she would never find the rooster. It was as hopeless as picking a star from the sky by poking it with a stick.

But our expedition to the village that night was a meaningful event to Mother. It must've been her first thorough exploration of the village since arriving on her wedding day.

Mother was tough enough to usually stay up all night sewing, but that night she seemed to become exhausted in the bitter coldness. I also gradually became weary of searching through bleak yards, yards containing only bundles of cornstalks standing with medicinal herbs spread over their tops to dry.

The wind howled through openings in papered doors and thick smoke rose from chimneys. The villagers were burning tree bark for heat and on the side of one of those chimneys jutting up from the ground we warmed our freezing hands. And this reminded me of Sam-rae.

"Mother," I called out.

"What?"

"Do you know where Sam-rae is now?"

This abrupt question must've surprised her. When she responded to it, her voice was low and tinged with irritation.

"We're looking for our rooster, not for Sam-rae."

"Sam-rae and I used to warm our hands just like this, and it brings back memories of her."

"Do you talk about everything that comes to mind? You should know that there are things that you need to keep to yourself."

"Sam-rae doesn't have a home village, right Mother?"

"Who said that? It's not so. Her home village is Gil-an, as you well know, so don't ask if she does."

"Isn't it something you made up?"

"Well, my home village is Gil-an, so her home is also Gil-an," explained Mother.

After warming our hands, we sneaked away. I saw Mother staggering with fatigue, saw her dejected face filled with disappointment, quite different from the beginning of our search when she was strong and determined. Soon she began heading for home.

When we were entering our yard, we heard a valiant cock's crow coming from somewhere in the village. Since it was so late at night, a time when all things in nature slept soundly, I heard it so clearly that it almost pierced my eardrums. After hearing it three more times, Mother suddenly stopped. When she spoke, her words were emotionally charged.

"Wait a minute, let's make another round. This rooster probably couldn't get into other peoples' chicken coops and must be roaming about somewhere."

These words made me so angry that I couldn't help shouting at her.

"What are you talking about? You go ahead, but I'm not coming!"

"Didn't you just hear a rooster crowing?" Mother asked, in an angry tone.

"I did, but so what?" I retorted.

"How can you still squeak like a pig after hearing the sounds?" she asked.

Right at that moment, I was strongly tempted to divulge my secret about our rooster. I knew that I could easily put an end to our painful search in the cold night by saying just a few words. But I soon changed my mind. Even though it was indeed cold and uncomfortable, I wanted to savor her failure a little longer. To fuel her anxiousness, I asked Mother, "So you think that's our rooster, huh?"

"Maybe not, but I know one thing for sure—that I wouldn't be able to sleep if I didn't make another effort after hearing the crowing," she said.

"Well, don't roosters crow in the early morning for no reason?" I replied.

Standing straight up, Mother didn't budge at all.

"Why did you buy the rooster? Don't we just need some hens for eggs?" I said.

"Don't you know that hens without a rooster lay unfertilized eggs?" she explained.

That night, after bumping into Chang-beom's mother, who had been looking for us with Ho-young on her back, my bittersweet pilgrimage through the village finally ended.

When we got home, each of us frozen like stones, it was almost dawn. As soon as we entered our cottage, Mother lay down at the warm part of the room. I then realized that the chicken must've meant more than just a mere rooster to Mother and that she felt a deep loss at its disappearance. Her pale lips and dragging movements revealed her frustration and despair.

Even in a warm and cozy room her appearance didn't change much. But she finally fell asleep, forgetting to hold Ho-young before she did. I regretted enjoying Mother's torment to the degree where even the cold weather didn't stop me. I still couldn't divulge what happened to the rooster, though.

When I woke up the following morning, Mother was in the yard. She was squatting in front of the chicken coop. I saw that she had already sprinkled grains on the ground for the hens but that they didn't come down from their rack to eat. They just couldn't leave when the rooster wasn't leading them.

Mother, with her doleful cooing sounds, continued trying to seduce the hens to step down to the yard. But instead, they moved further inside the chicken house and huddled up. So her idea of discovering the rooster's whereabouts by letting the hens free and following them didn't seem to be working. And so she eventually had to grab the hens, which were frantically running away from her, and carry them out of the chicken coop. But contrary to their usual habit, they only pecked on the grains several times and soon sneaked back into their coop and didn't budge from there.

Thwarted, Mother walked to the cold and empty porch while sighing heavily. And I realized that after the rooster disappeared, she didn't sit motionless in the warm part of the room with Ho-young on her bosom as much.

That evening it began snowing. Getting into the cottage after having delivered clothes to customers, Chang-beom's mother shook the snow off her shoulders. Realizing that it was snowing, Mother hastily flung open the door. She then said to herself,

"We'll never find the rooster if we have snow like this."

My heart melted.

"Do you think I should go out again to look for it?" I asked Mother.

Of course what I said was empty talk. But if it could offer her even a tiny bit of comfort, then I didn't mind saying it.

"I don't think it's necessary. He's also an animal with feet, so he'll come back when he wants to of his own free will," said Mother.

After casting a disagreeable glance at the falling snow, Mother closed the door. I could already feel a weighty air in the room, a sign that it would be quite a snowfall.

"It will probably snow a lot; I feel a heaviness in my chest," said Chang-beom's mother.

And as if confirming her weather forecast, the following morning we had snow up to my knees. It snowed so much that when I opened my eyes, I, without thinking, pushed open the hatch door to the kitchen. Yes, I thought of Sam-rae. It felt like she, having sneaked into the kitchen, was squatting there as she once did. I knew, though, such a wish wouldn't come true. But I also wished that Mother would forget about the rooster.

Three days had passed since I began waiting for the snow on the road to melt a bit so that I could go to town, and once it did, I was on my way. But when I left home, I had no clear plan, no idea what I was going to do.

The moon was very bright. Suddenly, my heart sank and a chill ran through my spine when I realized that I was walking alone on the road at night, even though I knew it wasn't that far. But the moonlight was illuminating the road almost as brightly as the sun and by singing to myself I soon overcame my fear. In no time my body was burning hot and steam billowed out of my mouth as I breathed.

I saw my shadow flickering in the moonlit snow. And in that moonlight, I saw Sam-rae.

Naked, she was threading softly towards me from the far end of the snow-covered road. *That must be either a ghost or a spook or maybe a nymph*, I thought. I shook my head, reasoning that ghosts should wear long white robes that cover their feet and that spooks should have horn-like lumps on their heads. And as for nymphs, they don't touch the ground when walking. And so it must be Sam-rae.

I believed that a wildflower-like woman, who never ceases to dream of blooming, even in the storms of the world, and who was proud and dignified while bearing a broken heart, must've walked naked in such a splendid moonlight.

Reflecting the moonlight bouncing off the snow, Sam-rae's body was a radiant white. I stopped walking and watched the bewitching sight of her. Yes, she came back to our village, I thought.

But something was strange. Behind Sam-rae was a vast millet field and farther back was a green rice field, endlessly spreading out to the horizon. It was absurd to see millet and green rice fields in the middle of winter. But I saw such an absurdity as being natural. I thought that whatever related to Sam-rae was right, even though a huge contradiction existed.

After standing there for a while, I soon resumed walking. Sam-rae and I walked for some time towards each other. Then something happened that I could never have imagined. The distance between us, which had seemed so short that I thought we were about to collide into each other in no time, didn't diminish at all. I walked so fast that I was breathing like a galloping horse on a winter day, but we still couldn't meet!

I became distressed and also apprehensive about whether what was happening to me was a sign of my freezing to death. It wasn't unusual to hear of drunken travelers or beggars freezing to death after becoming lost in a snowstorm or falling off a hilly, snowbound path.

Does it mean that Sam-rae had frozen to death and her ghost is appearing before me? Or who knows, maybe I'm seeing all this now because I'm dying. But I continued walking on, thinking that Sam-rae wasn't so dumb as to freeze to death. She was such an audacious woman, audacious enough to sneak into our kitchen like an alley cat, and so I thought my worrying was unnecessary.

Suddenly, Sam-rae got closer to me, only a few steps away now. But this time the word "Noo-na" didn't come out of my mouth. She also didn't call my name. *Are both of us ghosts then?*

Maybe it was true that we were meeting each other as ghosts. *But why then did she appear in front of me naked on this cold, snowy winter night?*

I finally called out her name loud enough that all my intestines and organs felt like they would pop out through my mouth. But she vanished without a trace, taking the millet and rice fields with her. All I saw was the snow-covered road lying wretchedly in the cold moonlight, a road that once had made me feel secure.

But even after she had disappeared, I didn't think it was a hallucination. I just thought that Sam-rae had run away from me.

Suddenly, Nu-rung-jy appeared out of nowhere and tugged at my trousers with his teeth. I smelled manure coming from him. I then realized that I was already near the village. Nu-rung-jy had heard my voice while rummaging in the snow nearby and had dashed over to me.

I stood there and didn't move in expectation that Sam-rae would reappear. And at the entrance to the alleyway to my house, I again stood motionless until I no longer could bear the biting coldness numbing my neck.

In the distance I saw light coming from my cottage. It looked dim in the bright moonlight. And I thought how it was always my cottage that was lit up late at night in the village.

The light looked like a red radish dangling in the moonlit night. For a moment the red radish ceased moving and remained still but soon appeared as if it was swaying while pushing away the moonlight, little by little. Nu-rung-jy shook the snow off his body before he and I began running home.

As I entered the cottage, Mother glanced at me and quietly said, "The night wind must be very cold. And I'm sure you've looked for the rooster."

But I didn't know how to respond to her, and I think it was then that I really saw the cozy and ordered room for the first time, the room that I once thought cold and strange.

"I finally found out what happened to our rooster," said Mother.

She said this with a heavy sigh, heavy enough to cave in the floor. I felt horrible, realizing that she finally discovered what had really happened to the chicken. Mother continued talking.

"I'm not sure if I should say this to you, a mere child, but I think I need to. If I close my mouth to save his honor, an innocent person, you, will suffer searching for the rooster in this cold weather every night. And if by any chance you caught a cold while doing so, who's going to make it up to you?" said Mother.

I finally managed to ask her a question.

"Did you find the rooster?"

"Yes, I did, but it doesn't matter now," she said.

Still standing up and feeling somewhat lost and empty, I looked down at my mother. But something was strange, in that Chang-beom's mother didn't add even a word while sitting with her back to us in silence. So I decided to wait for Mother to say whatever she had to. At that moment, Mother lowered her voice and began speaking.

"You might be surprised to hear this but I found a torn wing from our rooster next to Jang's jar stand; he must've dropped it while butchering the chicken. The feathers were still vivid and beautiful, as if they belonged to a living bird. And it seems that he buried it in the snow to hide the evidence, but the dishwater and bathwater thrown from his kitchen melted the snow and uncovered the wing. I never imagined that our neighbor would do such a terrible thing, killing and eating a neighbor's chicken! What do you think I should do about it?" asked Mother.

I saw Mother's eyes brimming with tears. Ever since I had become more aware of things, I'd never seen her with such a desperate face. But I didn't know what to do to comfort her.

It was a strange thing.

The very person who buried the chicken wing under the chimney of Jang's cottage and not next to his jar stand was me. And I couldn't understand how the buried wing got to our neighbor's jar stand in front of his kitchen. But I soon realized what I had done wrong. I remembered that when I buried it there, Nu-rung-jy was with me throughout the whole burying process.

"I feel like I got stabbed in the back. Thanks to this, I now clearly know what kind of neighbor we have; a man with a nice façade and seemingly concerned about his neighbor but who is in reality a cruel person. And though he had a wicked intention, how could he pretend not to know anything after killing and eating the rooster that I bought so that our hens don't lay rotten eggs? Remember this, my son—he's a bad man and we should ignore him," said Mother.

It was then that Chang-beom's mother, listening silently to her boss grumbling, finally turned around and told her, "Sister, maybe you should go to bed now. What can you do when the rooster is already dead? If you keep thinking about it, it'll only hurt you more. Why don't you go to town this coming market day and buy another rooster."

"Even if I rummage through this whole country, I won't find

such a good rooster, ever," said Mother.

"Who knows, you may find one, if you really look," said Chang-beom's mother.

"You know, you aren't really helping me by saying that, so why don't you stop meddling in our affairs," said Mother.

"But maybe his dog spotted the wing somewhere else and took it to his house, don't you think so? I doubt that a gentleman like Jang actually did such a thing, killing and eating a neighbor's chicken and then pretending innocence, just like a village bum," explained Chang-beom's mother.

"As they say, you can sound water ten fathoms deep but you can't sound the human heart a single fathom," said Mother.

"Well, I still can't believe it," said Chang-beom's mother.

"What do you mean *still can't believe* when the evidence is clear enough? You must want to upset me by saying that, don't you?"

Apparently, Mother's words discouraged her helper from siding with Jang any longer, since she suddenly stopped talking.

I felt an itch on my tongue. As a matter of fact, Jang didn't butcher our rooster to eat; it was his dog, Nu-rung-jy, that attacked and killed it. I discovered our chicken on Jang's manure pile. And next to it, I saw Nu-rung-jy with his snout all covered with blood. When I got close to the dog, it stopped biting on the chicken and hid his tail between his hind legs and ran away.

At first I didn't have any idea what to do. It was obvious what Nu-rung-jy would have to suffer if Mother discovered what had happened. She didn't like the dog from the beginning. So if I ever told her that it killed our rooster, she would never leave the dog in peace.

Picking up the still warm and bloody rooster, I hid it inside my jacket. I then went to the village bog and threw it in. And even after getting rid of the dead chicken, I still wasn't at ease, so

I went back to the manure heap and looked over every inch of the area.

It was then that I spotted a part of the rooster—the wing. I buried it in the ground with Nu-rung-jy watching me all the while, and once I left there, he must've dug it out and did what he had to do with it before flinging it next to Jang's jar stand.

The reason I tried to cover up the dog's crime with all my heart was because of my grudge against my mother and Ho-young. I was ecstatic and felt a deep camaraderie with the dog after he had done what I wanted to do—something that would upset my mother. That was how I became an accomplice to the crime.

And I believed that I did the right thing, since Nu-rung-jy had done what I didn't dare do. To be honest, I was so excited that I even wanted to hug the dog tightly and tumble around on the snow-covered ground with him. But the problem was that all the blame was aimed at my neighbor and I lost the chance to explain what had really happened.

As long as I kept silent, Jang would remain as bold as brass, a two-faced man of infamy to my mother. But I decided anyway never to tell her the truth. I thought that whatever happened between my mother and him, it wasn't my business.

Heartbroken, Mother didn't even leave the house for three days after that. But market day arrived. And so early in the morning we headed for town to look for another rooster to become our new family member. As before, when we had bought the now dead rooster, we leaned against the same wall in the sun at the market place and waited for it to open and become boisterous with people haggling and shouting. When it did open, we began to search for a rooster.

Mother considered the world as being some kind of filthy beachside flophouse, but regardless of this, she did return to the market place. It was unusual for her to once again go there and devote herself to searching for a rooster the whole day. But unfortunately, even after looking into every corner of the market, we still couldn't find a rooster resembling our old one. But she didn't easily give up.

In the drifting snow the market place was cold throughout the day. Only a few vendors were there, pacing around a bonfire, and I heard them say to each other that there weren't enough people to even stop their fighting if by any chance it happened. I was eager to get close to the bonfire, but Mother's stern eyes tried to keep me from even looking at it, so never mind my going there and mixing with the market people; I couldn't even get close to it.

Shivering in the bitter cold weather, we wandered about the market until the short winter day disappeared behind the mountain and dusk gathered around us. Exhausted, Mother finally dropped to the ground next to a mud wall covered with dead pumpkin stalks.

Vertigo had suddenly overcome her. With her eyes closed, she tried to gather herself together, and tears welled up when she finally opened her eyes. Muddy snow was piled up next to her. And her rear was already half buried in it, but she was too tired to even notice it.

"Mother, let's go home."

"Yes, let's go. I'm afraid that this absurd thing you and I have been doing all day might appear in your father's dreams. What a shameful thing we've been doing all day," said Mother.

"Why do you even mention father here? Aren't you buying a rooster just for Ho-young?"

I thought my words would hit a sensitive spot in her. They were words that I had kept inside me and didn't dare utter. And as I expected, she sensed the barbs in my words. Mother gazed at me for a while without saying anything. But what then came out of her mouth was something I hadn't expected.

"Listen, the reason I wanted to have a rooster at home wasn't for Ho-young but because I felt empty in my heart. Still being a baby unable to even speak, he's never nagged me for a rooster, right? You see, after losing the rooster, my mind was floating in the clouds and wasn't easy to rein in. If we didn't buy it, I wouldn't have this struggle. Yes, I shouldn't have gotten the rooster in the first place. It was a mistake," said Mother.

"If it was so special to you why then did you ask me to take care of it instead of you doing it?" I asked.

"I was afraid of the villagers gossiping if they ever saw me tending a male chicken with such care and tenderness," said Mother.

"I don't understand. What's wrong with you feeding a chicken?"

"I only wish people in the world would think the same as you do. But you see, so many grown-ups must sleep with dirty rags in their mouths, since they have such foul tongues," said Mother.

She then was about to get up and I tried to help her, but she motioned me away and managed to rise by herself while holding on to the wall. And I noticed that she left an impression on the snow larger than her actual rear-end. We left and only sparrows remained at the market place, chattering and pecking at grains on the frozen ground.

After leaving, we entered the main road and Mother turned around and motioned for me to lead the way. Walking in front of her, I listened to her monologue-like talk.

"I heard that countless people live in this world. For sure, I am one of them, but come to think of it, only two people really know me, a woman living in this lonely mountain village: you and your father. And it's amazing how many ups and downs I, as a mere woman, have to go through to just maintain this scanty existence. And it's disgraceful that I went to the market to buy another rooster to replace the one that's gone," said Mother.

I finally had a dim realization that her sorrow was somewhere deep inside her where I could never reach. And I knew that I couldn't get close to her sadness. Nothing I could do would console her, but if there was anything, it was to tell her the truth about our rooster.

I was torn, though, as to whether to tell her or not. But I finally decided not to, since it was horrible to even imagine the brutal punishment that Nu-rung-jy would receive. Maybe he wouldn't be killed, but for sure, he would suffer harsh beatings and more from Jang and my mother. So I couldn't put the dog in such a horrible situation. Going home, the snow on the road was all frozen and we proceeded on our way cautiously.

"Only after some time had passed since your father and I began living together," Mother said, "did I finally realize that I married a man without any particular occupation. I discovered that he was close to being a bum who had to rely on other people to even farm his own land, though he was a descendant of a once-good family. And he wasn't an educated man deserving the respect of others, either. Nor was he the kind of man who stayed home; no, every single day, rain or shine, without any exception, he had to go out, and once out, he used to get home after midnight and sometimes he didn't show up for three or four days in a row. But I couldn't complain about it. I just thought that men were supposed to be busy and it was only normal for him to act that way. Believing this, how could I think of complaining? I even encouraged your father to join the gambling sessions in the village and not just remain a bystander, sitting behind real men and only collecting the winners' tips. Don't you think that's what a man is supposed to do?"

I wasn't sure whether Mother was criticizing father or siding with him, but whatever, it was the very first time that she had ever talked to me about him in such detail and at such length.

I really didn't care about whether father was a bum or a farmer in name only. What was important and made my heart swell was that Mother confided in me for the first time about my father. I think it happened by chance that she opened herself up and talked about her husband, ending by saying something unexpected.

"It's an old story now, but do you know who hinted that your father was a bum hanging out at gambling sites? It was that scoundrel who ate up our rooster. If you know your friend's shortcomings, you should do your best to cover it up, but our neighbor isn't such a gentleman. He's such a base creature, talking about other people's weaknesses, so when I heard Chang-beom's mother saying that Jang was a gentleman, I was so dumbfounded that I couldn't find words to respond to such nonsense," said Mother.

While listening to her lambast Jang, I realized that her forgetting about the rooster was unlikely. When the following market day came, though, Mother didn't ask me to go there again. To relieve her anger against Jang, I thought she had to at least go to the market and buy another rooster, but she seemed to have totally forgotten about it. Or maybe something more urgent came up.

An even stranger thing than her apparently forgetting about the chicken was that she discreetly began to clean up the cottage. She took the comforter out of our built-in closet where it was stored for years and washed the covers and then spent a half day cleaning and arranging sauce jars. Following this, she coated the kitchen kiln with fresh mud when it really didn't need it and re-arranged the firewood in the backyard. With all her house chores, she didn't seem to have time to go the market and get another rooster.

Because of Mother's unusual behavior, I finally sensed that my father was coming home. I figured that Mother knew he was either near the village though still far away or heard that he was getting ready to return home. Whatever she had heard, if it wasn't something related to father, she wouldn't have driven herself, a woman isolated from the world for so long, into taking such action.

While moving around the house doing her chores, her face was beaming. I wondered when and who had brought the news of father's homecoming to Mother, and if that was really happening, then why did she keep it a secret even from me? Around that time, no one had come to our house nor did we receive any mail, either.

Five or six days had passed since Mother began house cleaning, and when most of the work was done, the event I had expected finally happened, though with a different person. The man who showed up after I had gone through days of tension over Mother's frantic behavior was her elder brother, who was living in Mother's home village, Gil-an, and not my father. When he gently pushed open the gate without making any sound after probably a long walk in the snow, I couldn't overcome the disappointment that was pricking my heart. He was the one who was quietly opposed to my mother marrying my father and who was supposed to help his suffering sister but didn't. When a short man entered the front yard late in the afternoon, I felt an uncontrollable urge to escape.

While he was exchanging greetings with Mother, I rushed out of the cottage. To be exact, I didn't run away from the cottage, I ran away from my uncle, whom I saw for the first time. Deep in my heart, I was angry at him, and this mingled with a mysterious sadness.

I saw my uncle's still fresh footsteps in the snow that covered the alleyway. I stepped on each of his footsteps backwards. The footsteps, the clear evidence that a visitor had come to our house, were nullified, one by one, under my footsteps. And I wished that his visit would be a futile one, as were his footprints.

I soon entered the main road. It was muddy and slushy, with only a few people to be seen. Previously, I had so many places to go once I left home, but that day in the early evening, I couldn't move; it was as if my legs were cut off.

The rice mill must've been closed by then. And it was lame to go out and pretend I was searching for an already-dead rooster. For a long time I gazed at the rolling mountain ridges, covered with swirling snow. The ridges rippled upward before vanishing in the grey sky.

It became bitterly cold. Suddenly, I looked down at my feet. And as I saw that I still had two solid legs, I started walking without thinking where I was going. I walked for I don't know how long, but I stopped when I realized where I was—standing in front of the tavern in town. But the room that had been always brightly lit at night was now dark. And there wasn't any trace of people inside, either, and the kitchen door, through which an old woman had always scurried in and out while cooking, was firmly shut. Since there wasn't even a dog around barking, the area was silent and looked deserted.

In an exaggerated manner I called out for anyone inside and got no response. Later, I threw stones into the yard but no one called out and this reassured me that the building was empty. In despair at feeling that everything related to Sam-rae had disappeared, I began shivering.

I closed my eyes. I felt like I was standing on top of a cliff where I didn't dare look down. Unless I became an eagle right then, a way to escape from my hopelessness didn't seem possible.

I knew that Sam-rae had left me forever. In front of the tavern I learned that a lit lamp, a mere sign that a place was open for business, could catapult me between hope and despair. But the lamp wasn't there any more. And I knew that everything between Mother and I, father and I, and Sam-rae and I, whether trivial or not, would vanish one day, just like the lamplight.

Being unable to move even one step forward from the cliff, I continued to shiver. I felt the ground collapsing beneath my feet. If I didn't fly off right then, I thought, I would fall tens of meters down and break into pieces. Suddenly, I felt thirsty and, without knowing what I was doing, began to eat the snow, white as a gourd flower. I ate so much of it and soon became so full that I dropped to the ground.

And of course, I wasn't on a cliff and I didn't transform into an eagle, either, and all because my belly was as big as a huge gourd. Resting on the ground, it suddenly dawned on me that I had enough information to find Sam-rae. It was my despair that had blocked me from remembering that I had hidden a paper with her address on it in the wall surrounding our house.

When I came home the room was lit but I didn't hear the sewing machine. Chang-beom's mother seemed to have left early. Quietly, I sat down on the porch.

"Don't worry about where I sleep tonight," my uncle said to my mother inside, "I've already arranged it for tonight with your neighbor, Jang; as you know, we've known each other for a long time. And to make it easy, Jang said his family is in Dae-goo and he's alone, so staying there one night was no problem."

"But brother, you came a long way to visit us. I can't let you stay at someone else's house," said Mother.

"Times have changed, so don't fret about it, and I'm fine wherever I stay. If it's not that big of a nuisance, there's nothing wrong in neighbors helping each other. Anyway, since your husband will soon return, please keep him under control and don't tarnish the family name again. Family life isn't anything else but living together under the same roof even though you have to go through ups and downs, often accompanied by the sounds of breaking jars, unless both of you have already decided to cut off the marital bond. That's life and that's how most people live. But what kind of living is it when a couple like you two are cold and indifferent to each other, just like an ox and a hen," said my uncle.

I went back to the gate and made out I was just arriving home and this stopped their conversation. My uncle opened the door. Looking surprised, he asked me as I was about to step onto the porch, "Where have you been at this late hour?"

But Mother answered him instead.

"Se-young has been sleepwalking nowadays."

Turning around to Mother, his eyes widened.

"What are you talking about? You must be kidding, huh?" asked my uncle.

"Don't worry, since it isn't serious," said Mother.

"Are you out of your mind? Who said it isn't serious?" he asked.

"I worried, too, and went to the doctor's office in town, and there everyone said that five or six out of ten teenage boys sleepwalk," said Mother.

"Are you saying that you visited the doctor but still didn't get any medication?" he asked Mother.

"They said it doesn't need any medication because it'll go away after a couple of months even without any treatment," said Mother.

"His father will be upset if he finds out about this," my uncle said.

"Don't worry, it'll pass," responded Mother.

I couldn't understand why she made up such a story. It could've been to defend me, I thought, but, at the same time, it sounded as if she was mocking me. As if I indeed was a sleepwalker, though, I didn't say a word about it and just entered the back room, my precious haven. But soon enough I heard Mother, saying, "Se-young, would you go with your uncle to Jang's cottage and help him with his bedding?"

"It isn't necessary. I'll go alone . . . it's just next door," said my uncle.

"Oh, no, that's not right. Se-young, what are you waiting for?"

My uncle and I began walking towards Jang's place. Once we got on the road, Jang's brightly lit cottage came into view. My uncle put his hand on my shoulder and said, "Se-young, I know you've been going through some tough times even though you're still young. Your sleepwalking must've happened because of it."

"I'm not a sleepwalker . . . Mother made it all up," I told him.

"Your mother wouldn't talk like that about her precious son if he were perfectly fine. Maybe you aren't aware of it but sleepwalking is common among boys your age. Anyway, once your father comes home, it'll be taken care of; he'll take you to a doctor for an accurate diagnosis. Even though you don't have anything, it's about time for you to see a doctor and get a checkup, anyway," said my uncle.

It was strange that I was so calm even though the grown-ups were saying that father would soon be returning home. My memories of him were all distant and barren, but the grown-ups were all excited, acting as though they would celebrate his homecoming as some kind of an important event.

But to me, someone used to being alone and unfamiliar with the ways of people, all of this was rather a huge and unsolvable riddle. Maybe I was feeling more dizziness and disillusion with the coming event than anticipation or excitement.

I had searched for any reason to hate Mother, since I missed having a father a lot and had roamed aimlessly about on the embankment following his mirage. But I had no idea how to relate to him and didn't have any rosy plan about what to do when he came home. I then finally saw that the image I had of my father was false. So I was feeling more afraid and dizzy than happy and excited in my dim and confused state of mind.

Hearing our footsteps on the frozen snow as we entered the yard, Jang opened the door and greeted us. Stepping inside, we saw a low table with rice wine and kimchi on it in the middle of the room. The two men exchanged a litany of greetings and then sat on the floor with the table between them.

Since my uncle hadn't told me to go back home, I also had to sit down. From the table Jang picked up a kettle filled with rice wine with one hand and a porcelain bowl with the other and poured the milky white drink to the rim of the bowl. He then handed it to my uncle who suddenly motioned to me and said, "Se-young, come closer here."

Startled and bewildered, I immediately did what I was told. My uncle then spoke, but his words seemed to be aimed at Jang, not me.

"Se-young, you're the eldest son of your family. And that means you represent it and bear comparison with us men until your father returns. So here, you have the first drink," said my uncle, holding the bowl out in front of me.

It was a totally unexpected suggestion and I was baffled. Wanting to hide myself, even in a rat hole if there were any, I withdrew from them and sat against a wall. But the situation wasn't that simple.

Now even Jang began to egg me on. Unable to shake off the two pushy men, I finally took the bowl and started sipping the rice wine. It was my first time drinking alcohol; even though I was curious about what being drunk was like, alcohol had been something inaccessible to me.

Finally, my uncle said that I could leave. As I hurriedly got out of the room, Nu-rung-jy, who had been waiting under the porch, followed me. Once outside, I didn't want to go directly home after having my first drink.

Like a colt on a loosened rein, I roamed aimlessly about everywhere in the village. Under the bright moon, the village was silent. Nu-rung-jy tagged along, making crunching sounds on the frozen snow as he did.

In no time I was on the embankment near the stream. I saw a white birch tree standing alone at the north end of the embankment. With its snow-white bark, the birch didn't grow as quickly as a poplar tree, which every year adds a visible length of growth. The tree appeared stately, though, resembling a kneeling person at the edge of a cliff.

What stood dignified wasn't only the white birch tree. The zelkova trees at the village entrance and poplars along the embankment looked the same in the harsh winter gusts.

It was something new when I noticed the kneeling white birch, something that had never before attracted my attention. I remembered that one time I saw villagers siphon the tree's sap through holes they had drilled at its base. And as soon as this scene came into my mind, I suddenly felt that my bladder was full and about to burst at any moment. Any pressure on my abdomen at all, and I would have peed myself.

I unbuttoned my pants and, aiming at the birch tree, shot a stream of pee and then straightened up my clothes. Afterwards, I cupped my hands around my mouth and shouted towards the direction of the village, "You son of a bitches, listen! My father's coming back!"

I did this not because I was happy that my father was coming home but rather because I wanted to let people know that I was no longer fatherless and so could speak and act the way other boys did. I yelled out a couple of more times until I finally felt a needling coldness and my empty stomach.

When I came home, Mother was sleeping soundly, with Ho-young on her bosom. Chang-beom's mother, working alone at the sewing machine, scolded me for roaming about so late. I saw that she was busily making Ho-young's clothes.

I lay down in the room. I felt fatigue penetrating my bones. It was the first night in a while that I had such a sweet sleep, my weariness spreading into my flesh like a heat wave.

Mother's welcoming preparations for father resumed the following day. She began this second round by changing the wallpaper in the room.

She went to town with Chang-beom's mother and returned with rolls of blush pink wallpaper, patterned with dandelion flowers. With bundles of wallpaper rolls on their heads, the two women came home after walking proudly through the village.

The next day, Mother and I began to paper the walls. First, I spread glue evenly on the backside of the paper and Mother, with Ho-young on her back, then held it up and layered it onto the old discolored paper. The room was soon filled with the smell of glue, and Ho-young whimpered whenever Mother bent down and squeezed him.

The old paper was grayish black, dirtied with dust and stains and smoke from the lamp. One by one, as we covered up each strip of the old wallpaper, the room became brighter and brighter, looking like water with the sun shining through it. There was a paperhanger in the village but Mother didn't seem to want help from anyone. So even after we worked all day, more than half of the paper still needed to be hung.

But repairing the outer wall wasn't something Mother and I could do without any help. So Mother sent me to Jang. When I got to the rice mill, he was gambling in the room where his workers lived. Noticing I was there, he came to me while dragging his rubber shoes.

"What brings you here in this cold weather?" he asked.

"My mother told me to ask you to look for someone to help us fix our wall."

Neither of us said a word, though both of us moved to the sunny corner of the mill anyway.

"Are you sure your mother sent you here?" he asked.

"Yes," I answered.

He took out a cigarette from his pocket and held it between his lips. I suddenly saw that he was no longer as friendly as before, standing with an indifferent and haughty face. He lit his cigarette and deeply sucked on it a couple of times before dropping it to the ground and stepping on it.

He then was silent, but as time passed, his face clearly revealed that he didn't welcome Mother's request. As usual, he crisscrossed his arms and gazed at the main road in front of the mill, but finally said in a gloomy voice, "You see, your father will be home in several days . . . and I don't understand why your mother had to ask me. For sure, once your father's home he'll take care of everything."

It was the very first time that Jang was that indifferent towards a matter that concerned my mother.

Tinged with some exaggeration, he had always made a great effort to treat Mother and me warmly, regardless of my mother's coldness and indifference to him. Previously, the more Mother became indifferent to him, the more eager he became to please and help her, never even hesitating once. And he was the only one who had expressed his concern about my father not returning home and who had shown his heartfelt sympathy for my mother.

But now he was speaking ill of my father.

"I'm not sure if I should say this to you, but even if a man, who has wandered about and lived a rootless and irresponsible life, comes home, it wouldn't necessarily mean he had changed. And who knows what trouble he'll cause once he's back home. Sorry for saying this, but you must know, too, that your father isn't in a position where he can stride proudly back, is he? And by the way, was it your mother who contacted your uncle with information about your father's whereabouts and asked him to arrange his return?" he asked.

"That I don't know," I answered.

"It's hard to understand why your mother has to accept this man back, a man who hasn't even contacted her for such a long time. Something is wrong here. And are you saying that you don't know how your uncle found out about your father?"

"I don't have the slightest idea," I said.

I couldn't understand why his attitude towards us had to suddenly change. *Does he have a grudge against my father like I have against my mother? But why? And if so, where did all his concerns and caring for us come from before?*

Without waiting for his answer, I left Jang's mill and entered the main road. I felt a burning shame at the back of my neck, as if I had been kicked there. My eyes became blurry with tears. I couldn't figure out what I was feeling then; it was a kind of guilt as well as a release from something that had blocked my heart for so long. Tears, thick as pine resin, ran down my cheeks.

And of course, I didn't divulge Jang's coldness to my mother but only said that he had declined her request. She attentively listened to my words, but something was strange; she didn't look like she was disturbed at Jang's refusal, and, furthermore, she didn't even criticize him, either. For some reason, she seemed to take it in stride. And so it fell on Chang-beom's mother to search for a handyman.

As the wall repair job began, the whole house was in a hectic state in preparation for my father's return. But in the middle of the commotion, I kept thinking about what Jang had asked me.

Who plotted all these schemes? Who contacted my uncle, a man who had stopped seeing his sister for such a long time, as if harboring an old hatred? Who moved this man to arrange my father's return?

I knew for sure that Mother couldn't have done such a thing.

But, at the same time, I also knew that she had waited for father the last six years and that it was a painful period.

I was the one, though, who understood very well that Mother's waiting was allowing my father to waste his life away. But I didn't have the wisdom and reasoning power of grown-ups, who were even capable of deciphering the lives of ancient people from mere earthenware found in old tombs.

What I knew were things like when a bridal wreath tree would sprout or when it's a good time to make a flute out of willow tree bark. And as a boy interested only in such things, I naturally failed to figure out who was responsible for what was happening. It was like seeing strange footprints—they clearly existed, but I had no idea who they belonged to.

During that period Ho-young was particularly peevish and so, at night, Mother had to do her sewing with the whimpering baby on her back. She didn't want anyone else to make father's new clothes; she wanted to make them by herself. And being cross about this, Chang-beom's mother tossed about sharp barbs, but Mother didn't really care.

The next thing Mother did was to inspect all the huge sauce and paste jars, something she hadn't done in a long time. She meticulously inspected each jar and made sure the contents tasted right before leaving the lids off to sterilize the sauce and paste in the sun. But regardless of her fussy preparation and nervousness, father still seemed far away. Mother, though, didn't express her feelings to me at all.

Her calm demeanor resembled that of a duck floating on water, one that looked serene and elegant in water, as if effortlessly gliding on the surface, but who in reality was vigorously paddling to keep moving.

It seemed to me that Mother and Jang were infected with the same kind of internal affliction.

As the crumbling part of the wall was fixed and a new thatched roof was laid on top of it, the view of Jang's house, which before was almost a complete one from our porch, was considerably diminished. To me, the higher wall revealed what Mother was thinking: If only father returned home, she wouldn't mind cutting the connection with Jang, the only neighbor that she had any relationship with.

It was when the work on the wall was near completion that Jang was waiting for me when I passed by in front of his cottage. He took me inside and asked me to sit down.

"Sorry if it sounds like I'm intruding, but do you know when your father will arrive?"

"I don't know," I answered.

"Well, it's hard to imagine that your mother didn't say anything to you, the eldest son of the family, about his homecoming. She must've talked to you in detail about it."

"No, she didn't."

Being eager to hear anything, Jang glared at me. I even sensed a hostility in his eyes that I had never experienced before. I tried hard to look away from his sharp gaze before finally staring at the black and white family photo hanging on the wall. This inattentive attitude of mine must've rubbed him the wrong way. Clearing his throat, he pressed me further.

"I know that your mother is a callous person but I never knew she could so easily abandon her motherly obligation like this. If she didn't tell you when your father is returning home, what is it but deserting her parental duty?"

In his family photo, people with thin bodies were all smiling awkwardly, as if they were forced to do so by being whipped.

People in the back row had their hands on the shoulders of those in the front row. It looked like a staged photo intended to show off their family bond—a bond that in reality seemed to be crumbling and barely holding them together.

Where are all the smiling people of this family now? I had seen the woman in it several times and thought it was Jang's wife, but whenever I saw her, we passed by each other and never exchanged any words. Mother must've seen her more often than I did, but it didn't seem that the two women had a warm neighborly relationship. While looking at the photo, I thought that maybe I would soon enter a new world where I didn't have to relate to people who smiled in such a contrived manner.

"I should've asked your uncle if he knew when your father will be returning," said Jang. "But as the saying goes, it's not my business whether you offer a pear or a persimmon to your ancestors' ghosts; yes, I shouldn't interfere with your family matters. And I knew that a chance existed of being misinterpreted by your uncle if I had ever asked him about your father, so I didn't, but now I know it was a mistake. I don't understand why it should be such a big secret, so much so that your mother has to keep it to herself and not even tell you, her son. So you're sure then that you know nothing, huh? Well, I have other ways to find out."

I wasn't certain but I thought I knew what his strategy was. Since Chang-beom's mother by then was almost living with us day and night, he was no doubt going to talk to her and dig up whatever information he could. But his plan seemed so clumsy that I didn't think he would succeed.

But, nonetheless, his words piqued my curiosity; I was also dying to know when my father would come home. I realized that if I kept close watch of Jang I'd discover when my father would return, and this excited me. Knowing he wouldn't be able to wring any information from me, Jang let me leave, and once I was free of his inquisitive eyes, I began closely watching Chang-beom's mother, whom I knew Jang would contact.

After midnight, with her silk scarf wrapped around her neck, Mother's helper left our cottage. Fortunately, as she left, Mother, who was exhausted, was fast asleep with Ho-young still on her back. Apparently not wanting to wake up anyone, Chang-beom's mother quietly said good night to me before leaving.

Some time later, I sneaked out of our cottage through the kitchen door and followed Mother's helper, who was about to exit our alleyway. Jang's cottage, now blocked from our sight by the new high wall, was dark.

Chang-beom's mother scurried towards the main road. Her place was at the end of a long alleyway across from the road. Arriving at an empty lot near there, she suddenly stopped. She then lifted up her scarf a bit and studied the surroundings. Even though it was a busy main road during the day, it was unreasonable to expect to see anyone at that time.

It was right then that she turned around and began walking back. I quickly hid myself behind a manure pile and she, without noticing me, hurried back towards our cottage. But as I had expected, she soon entered Jang's yard.

How she got into his place, though, wasn't something that I could've imagined. Once she arrived at Jang's gate, she stopped and looked swiftly around. Making sure that she saw no one, she then tiptoed onto the porch and took off her shoes and hid them inside her skirt before entering his cottage.

While she was doing all this, the cottage was still dark and there wasn't any indication that Jang was inside. And even more strange was the fact that he hadn't locked the door. *Did she enter somebody's empty house?* The cottage was quiet and there wasn't a sign of anyone inside; I was baffled.

Another strange thing was Nu-rung-jy under the porch, supposedly guarding the place. Not only didn't he bark at Chang-beom's mother, but before going back under the porch, the dog even wagged his tail at her when she entered the cottage, entering without making a sound, just like smoke.

I wondered if, in order to exchange information about Mother or father, it was necessary for them to meet in such an odd way. Even after she got into the cottage, I didn't see any light on or hear any words coming from inside. What I could hear was only bustling sounds, like people hurriedly moving about.

I hid myself under the porch and then tightly hugged Nu-rung-jy's neck. Right then, the wood above my head began squeaking. It wasn't only the porch that was shaking; it seemed that the doorknob was also rattling. For a moment I was afraid that the whole house would collapse.

Quickly, as if flying, I crawled out from under the porch. I stood in the yard, far enough away from the cottage to have a full view of it.

There I finally heard them talking. I sneaked back under the porch.

"It looks like I'm poking my nose into somebody else's business," said Jang, "but I asked Se-young today when his father is coming home, but this kid didn't know anything about his own father."

"She wouldn't tell her son about such details, a young boy," replied Chang-beom's mother.

"Oh yes? Then she must've told you, since you're not a kid, right?" said Jang.

"She's so prim and keeps things to herself," Mother's helper said.

"Is it such a big secret that she doesn't even tell you?" asked Jang.

"Never mind me, she didn't even tell her own son. If you're dying to know that much, why don't you ask her directly, and if you don't want to do it, then forget about it. He'll come when he comes, and by the way, why are you so interested? What do you have to do with it? Are you going to town to greet him instead of his wife and son?" said Chang-beom's mother.

"Of course, I'm not. But as an old friend as well as a good neighbor, I'm just curious when he'll be coming back," said Jang.

"Stop talking nonsense. Do you think I don't know what's going on?" sneered Chang-beom's mother.

"What are you talking about?"

"Well, the rumor has spread throughout the whole village, so it's no use acting ignorant. Have you ever seen smoke coming out of a chimney without a fire going? Give me one example if you've ever seen anything without its cause. It's you who needs to confide in me, not the reverse," retorted Chang-beom's mother.

"I've been a good neighbor, offering a helping hand whenever she needed it, in spite of the danger of rumors spreading, since I felt sorry for her, a woman unfortunate enough to have a bum for a husband and who had to live like a widow. So whatever you heard, it's not true," said Jang.

"You aren't innocent . . . get your hands off of me," said Chang-beom's mother.

Under the porch I could hear clearly what the two had said. And what made it possible was that Mother's helper had a hearing problem and so they had to raise their voices, seemingly without realizing it.

What disappointed me the most was Jang, who had flattered me by saying I was my family's eldest son, speaking ill of me, calling me "that kid." And Chang-beom's mother wasn't much different, either; she sarcastically called my mother "prim." And all this made me feel that we'd been betrayed.

As usual, early the following morning Mother's helper came to our cottage. But there was no trace on her face of what had happened between her and Jang the previous night.

On the afternoon of the fourth day following the incident, Mother began changing her clothes. But her new clothes weren't the usual white ones; this time she put on a colored *chi-ma* and *jeo-go-ri*. From the scrupulous way she dressed herself, I finally sensed my father's shadow.

She put on rubber shoes, which she had washed snow white and dried in the sun. Following this, she asked me to accompany her. When we reached the end of our alleyway, she finally said, "Your father is coming today."

Afterwards, she remained silent all the way into town.

Mother's white rubber shoes shined whiter on the snow-covered road, and while walking she only stepped on the snow in order not to dirty her shoes in the mud. At one point I had a strong urge to confess something to her. Such an urge was totally unexpected and I had no idea from where it came.

I could've told her about what had taken place between Jang and Chang-beom's mother or that it was Nu-rung-jy who killed our rooster. I even came close to telling her that I had a paper with Sam-rae's address written on it hidden in a hole in our wall. But Mother's total silence prevented me from saying anything.

At the dried fish store, located at the entrance to town, Mother finally stopped walking. There she bought a stingray that was covered with dust. She meticulously brushed the dust off and then wrapped it with a cloth she had brought with her. We then headed for the bus stop, located at the west end of town. There, in the freezing cold, we waited for the day's last bus to arrive.

As it was approaching dusk, the main road that passed through town became dim. And it was desolate. For a long time our eyes were fixed at the east end of the main road where the bus would appear.

Freezing, I began shivering. *My hands are in my pockets but what should I do with them when I meet my father? Should I put them behind my back? Or should I hold them in front of me? Or do I put them inside the waist of my trousers?*

Yes, in the ritual surrounding my father's arrival, the most troublesome thing was where to place my hands while meeting him; I became restless. Mother stood motionless near me, her cheeks flushed; she must've sensed the ground rumbling even before the bus appeared.

From the far end of the main road a bus was making its slow and hesitant way towards us. When it stopped, I saw ten or so passengers inside. They soon got off the bus and one of them was my father. Mother, with her trembling hand, pointed to one of the travelers and then pushed me towards him, saying, "That's your father. Go greet him."

But I couldn't immediately move. I just stood there until she repeated what she had just said.

I recognized that I was in the very situation that I didn't want to be in. I had done many things for Mother, but this awkward greeting was something that I really wanted to avoid. But she asked me to greet him and so I had no other choice but to walk up to the man she had pointed to.

Without saying a word, I bowed to a neatly dressed man in a suit. At the moment he spotted me, he appeared flustered. But he quickly regained his composure after seeing Mother.

"It's you Se-young," he said.

After saying that, he patted me once on my head. For no apparent reason, I felt a lump in my throat and tears welled up and filled my eyes. He handed his carry-on bundle to me and then walked to Mother, who was fixed at her spot, and exchanged some words with her before coming back to me.

"Let's go," he said.

And then a strange procession began; I was at the head of it with the bundle followed by father four or five steps away, and Mother following five or six steps behind him.

It was late February and snow was still falling. The sun had already set, but it was still bright out, with snow piled everywhere and the weather mild.

I was unusually hungry and also thirsty, so I stuck out my tongue and moistened my mouth. Swirling in the wind, snowflakes, landing on my tongue, looked like dandelion seeds. While unbuttoning my jacket, I noticed that I had become even thirstier. And dandelion seeds were now beginning to fall on my chest.

In no time I was flying in the air like a dandelion seed. And it wasn't only me who was flying but also my father and mother. Having taken off all of our padded clothes and silk scarves without any hesitation, we were now all naked. But I wasn't cold, since the sun enveloped us within its warm beams.

Right then, a strange thing happened. I saw gray clouds rolling along the ground where only moments before warm sunrays had showered down. With this change of weather, our delightful flight became turbulent.

At that instant I saw one of Mother's white rubber shoes fall off her foot and begin its long journey to the ground. They were the shoes that Mother had decided to wear the day father came, and when I saw her shoe fall, I was so surprised that I suddenly stopped walking. But I soon picked up my speed because I didn't want my father to get closer to me. Most of all, I was afraid that he would begin talking. I was still feeling the embarrassment I felt when I met him at the bus stop.

Until we arrived at the entrance to the village, the distance between us hadn't changed. It was as if we had walked from town to our cottage in order to see whether the space between us would change or not.

When we arrived at home, I found that Mother was holding a handful of wild lettuce. Sprouting in winter through layers of snow, it was an herb that she often picked and rinsed in icy water before eating raw. She must've gotten them while walking home.

Father entered the brightly lit room, strutting in without any reservation. After he sat down, Mother's behavior was something I never expected. As though a newly wed bride, she respectfully kowtowed to him. She wore a white *jeo-go-ri* and a pale blue *chi-ma*, with the *chi-ma*'s ample volume ballooning out as she kneeled to bow. Lowering her head down further, her delicate nose looked sharper than usual.

Mother then hurriedly went to the kitchen, leaving father, who was wearing an awkward expression, in the room. She had already prepared dishes before going to town to meet him, so all she had to do was to heat up the food. Soon a nicely prepared dinner was ready. Father picked up his silver spoon, but instead of eating anything, he glanced at me, kneeling at the cold part of the room, and made an unexpected comment while pointing to me with his chin, "Well, you're still cross-eyed, I see."

He didn't have a trace of the village dialect, but Mother acted as if she heard nothing. Unexpectedly, painful memories returned, memories that I had stored at the edge of oblivion and tried to forget.

Was it because I missed my father? Was it father that caused me to see the dried stingray Mother hung on the doorsill as a ray-kite? Was it father that made Sam-rae's face look like a yellow poppy flower when lit up by match flames? Was it him that made me believe I saw a snow castle in the Himalaya Mountains? Was it him that made me wait for Jang to fish out a salmon from his bathtub? And was it him that caused the mill workers to look like grizzly bears?

Those very words father uttered that evening bit through the wings of a fourteen-year-old boy's dream and ripped it to pieces, just like Nu-rung-jy had done to our rooster. I stood up quietly and went into the back room to lie down, hunched over on my side. Tears wet my cheeks and I soon fell asleep.

I woke up late the following morning. I saw father sleeping and also saw an empty unruffled spot next to him. When I walked by, a sweet aroma radiated from the bedding.

In order not to wake up father, I tiptoed across the room and quietly opened the door and stepped on the porch. It was dazzling white outside. The whole world had been covered with the night's snow, and trees at the foot of the mountain were blooming with splendid snow flowers that looked like magnolias blossoming lavishly in early spring.

Snow was heaped up in the yard, in the alleyway, and on the wall's newly repaired top, as if someone last night had poured sacks of snow on them before running away. I thought that father could've been the snow envoy dispatched from the snow palace. It was just too much snow to be coincidence.

I soon noticed footsteps beginning from outside the alleyway and passing through our yard before ending right under our porch. They were the footsteps of someone coming to our house, but I didn't see any footsteps leaving. It was the very trick Sam-rae used to play when she had gone hunting with me for sparrows inside thatched roofs. I thought that only she knew the silly trick of camouflaging an outgoing visitor as an incoming one, but in fact, there was another person who knew it. I took a closer look at the snow-covered yard but still couldn't see any sign of someone having left.

Instantly, something flashed across my mind. Alert and wide awake, I ran to the back of the house in my bare feet. I then put my hand into the hole in the wall that I once thought only I knew about. I stretched my arm all the way in and searched inside, but the paper was gone, the paper with Sam-rae's address on it that the bar girl had written down with her eyebrow pencil.

Yes, Mother must've known everything; she even knew about my visit to the tavern and my getting Sam-rae's address.

Mother stole Sam-rae from me; she needed her in order to leave father. Her footprints, which she had camouflaged as incoming ones, were Mother's way of telling me, and not my father, that she would never return home. *But what made her decide to leave the morning following father's homecoming?*

Did she realize that all her hopes and dreams, harbored in her heart for six years, were illusions after seeing the bright new world created by the night's snowfall? Did she finally realize that all her beliefs were mere shadows shimmering on the wall? Did she realize that her pride and dignity had been trampled on and that her love, which she had sustained with her tears for all those years, was nothing but a delusion? Did she decide to discard her humiliating life and to embrace an adventurous one in a passionate new world?

I was sure that Mother wouldn't come back, but this didn't make me despair at all.

Just like Sam-rae showed that her heart had never left us by arranging my father's return with my uncle, I showed that I had never forgotten her by memorizing her address.

Glossary of Korean Terms

A-gung-y: the opening to a long tunnel-like kiln that Koreans used for cooking and heating floors

Bu-tu-mak: a raised earthen platform in the traditional Korean kitchen where cooking cauldrons are located

Chi-ma: a traditional Korean long skirt

Han-bok: traditional Korean clothing

Jeo-go-ri: a traditional Korean blouse

Ji-gae: an A-frame wooden back carrier

KIM JOO-YOUNG was born in 1939, and graduated from the Sorabol Art College, majoring in creative writing. He made his literary debut with *Resting Stage*, which won the 1971 New Writer's Award. A leading and popular exponent of "documentary" fiction set in meticulously researched historical periods, Kim has also served as the director of the Paradise Culture Foundation in Seoul since 2005.

INRAE YOU VINCIGUERRA AND LOUIS VINCIGUERRA have co-translated several Korean novels and short stories into English. Translator, teacher, and artist Inrae You Vinciguerra graduated from Seoul National University of Education. Louis Vinciguerra is an artist, teacher, and playwright who earned an MA degree in history from the University of California, Berkeley.

The Library of Korean Literature

The Library of Korean Literature, resulting from a collaboration between Dalkey Archive Press and the Literature Translation Institute of Korea, presents modern classics of Korean literature in translation, featuring the best Korean authors from the late modern period through to the present day. The Library aims to introduce the intellectual and aesthetic diversity of contemporary Korean writing to English-language readers. The Library of Korean Literature is unprecedented in its scope, with Dalkey Archive Press publishing 25 Korean novels and short story collections in a single year.

The series is published in cooperation with the Literature Translation Institute of Korea, a center that promotes the cultural translation and worldwide dissemination of Korean language and culture.

MICHAL AJVAZ, *The Golden Age.*
  The Other City.
PIERRE ALBERT-BIROT, *Grabinoulor.*
YUZ ALESHKOVSKY, *Kangaroo.*
FELIPE ALFAU, *Chromos.*
  Locos.
IVAN ÂNGELO, *The Celebration.*
  The Tower of Glass.
ANTÓNIO LOBO ANTUNES, *Knowledge of Hell.*
  The Splendor of Portugal.
ALAIN ARIAS-MISSON, *Theatre of Incest.*
JOHN ASHBERY AND JAMES SCHUYLER, *A Nest of Ninnies.*
ROBERT ASHLEY, *Perfect Lives.*
GABRIELA AVIGUR-ROTEM, *Heatwave and Crazy Birds.*
DJUNA BARNES, *Ladies Almanack.*
  Ryder.
JOHN BARTH, *LETTERS.*
  Sabbatical.
DONALD BARTHELME, *The King.*
  Paradise.
SVETISLAV BASARA, *Chinese Letter.*
MIQUEL BAUÇÀ, *The Siege in the Room.*
RENÉ BELLETTO, *Dying.*
MAREK BIEŃCZYK, *Transparency.*
ANDREI BITOV, *Pushkin House.*
ANDREJ BLATNIK, *You Do Understand.*
LOUIS PAUL BOON, *Chapel Road.*
  My Little War.
  Summer in Termuren.
ROGER BOYLAN, *Killoyle.*
IGNÁCIO DE LOYOLA BRANDÃO,
  Anonymous Celebrity.
  Zero.
BONNIE BREMSER, *Troia: Mexican Memoirs.*
CHRISTINE BROOKE-ROSE, *Amalgamemnon.*
BRIGID BROPHY, *In Transit.*
GERALD L. BRUNS, *Modern Poetry and the Idea of Language.*
GABRIELLE BURTON, *Heartbreak Hotel.*
MICHEL BUTOR, *Degrees.*
  Mobile.
G. CABRERA INFANTE, *Infante's Inferno.*
  Three Trapped Tigers.
JULIETA CAMPOS,
  The Fear of Losing Eurydice.
ANNE CARSON, *Eros the Bittersweet.*
ORLY CASTEL-BLOOM, *Dolly City.*
LOUIS-FERDINAND CÉLINE, *Castle to Castle.*
  Conversations with Professor Y.
  London Bridge.
  Normance.
  North.
  Rigadoon.
MARIE CHAIX, *The Laurels of Lake Constance.*
HUGO CHARTERIS, *The Tide Is Right.*
ERIC CHEVILLARD, *Demolishing Nisard.*

MARC CHOLODENKO, *Mordechai Schamz.*
JOSHUA COHEN, *Witz.*
EMILY HOLMES COLEMAN, *The Shutter of Snow.*
ROBERT COOVER, *A Night at the Movies.*
STANLEY CRAWFORD, *Log of the S.S. The Mrs Unguentine.*
  Some Instructions to My Wife.
RENÉ CREVEL, *Putting My Foot in It.*
RALPH CUSACK, *Cadenza.*
NICHOLAS DELBANCO, *The Count of Concord.*
  Sherbrookes.
NIGEL DENNIS, *Cards of Identity.*
PETER DIMOCK, *A Short Rhetoric for Leaving the Family.*
ARIEL DORFMAN, *Konfidenz.*
COLEMAN DOWELL,
  Island People.
  Too Much Flesh and Jabez.
ARKADII DRAGOMOSHCHENKO, *Dust.*
RIKKI DUCORNET, *The Complete Butcher's Tales.*
  The Fountains of Neptune.
  The Jade Cabinet.
  Phosphor in Dreamland.
WILLIAM EASTLAKE, *The Bamboo Bed.*
  Castle Keep.
  Lyric of the Circle Heart.
JEAN ECHENOZ, *Chopin's Move.*
STANLEY ELKIN, *A Bad Man.*
  Criers and Kibitzers, Kibitzers and Criers.
  The Dick Gibson Show.
  The Franchiser.
  The Living End.
  Mrs. Ted Bliss.
FRANÇOIS EMMANUEL, *Invitation to a Voyage.*
SALVADOR ESPRIU, *Ariadne in the Grotesque Labyrinth.*
LESLIE A. FIEDLER, *Love and Death in the American Novel.*
JUAN FILLOY, *Op Oloop.*
ANDY FITCH, *Pop Poetics.*
GUSTAVE FLAUBERT, *Bouvard and Pécuchet.*
KASS FLEISHER, *Talking out of School.*
FORD MADOX FORD,
  The March of Literature.
JON FOSSE, *Aliss at the Fire.*
  Melancholy.
MAX FRISCH, *I'm Not Stiller.*
  Man in the Holocene.
CARLOS FUENTES, *Christopher Unborn.*
  Distant Relations.
  Terra Nostra.
  Where the Air Is Clear.
TAKEHIKO FUKUNAGA, *Flowers of Grass.*
WILLIAM GADDIS, *J R.*
  The Recognitions.

FOR A FULL LIST OF PUBLICATIONS, VISIT:
www.dalkeyarchive.com

JANICE GALLOWAY, *Foreign Parts.*
    The Trick Is to Keep Breathing.
WILLIAM H. GASS, *Cartesian Sonata*
    and Other Novellas.
    Finding a Form.
    A Temple of Texts.
    The Tunnel.
    Willie Masters' Lonesome Wife.
GÉRARD GAVARRY, *Hoppla! 1 2 3.*
ETIENNE GILSON,
    The Arts of the Beautiful.
    Forms and Substances in the Arts.
C. S. GISCOMBE, *Giscome Road.*
    Here.
DOUGLAS GLOVER, *Bad News of the Heart.*
WITOLD GOMBROWICZ,
    A Kind of Testament.
PAULO EMÍLIO SALES GOMES, *P's Three*
    Women.
GEORGI GOSPODINOV, *Natural Novel.*
JUAN GOYTISOLO, *Count Julian.*
    Juan the Landless.
    Makbara.
    Marks of Identity.
HENRY GREEN, *Back.*
    Blindness.
    Concluding.
    Doting.
    Nothing.
JACK GREEN, *Fire the Bastards!*
JIŘÍ GRUŠA, *The Questionnaire.*
MELA HARTWIG, *Am I a Redundant*
    Human Being?
JOHN HAWKES, *The Passion Artist.*
    Whistlejacket.
ELIZABETH HEIGHWAY, ED., *Contemporary*
    Georgian Fiction.
ALEKSANDAR HEMON, ED.,
    Best European Fiction.
AIDAN HIGGINS, *Balcony of Europe.*
    Blind Man's Bluff
    Bornholm Night-Ferry.
    Flotsam and Jetsam.
    Langrishe, Go Down.
    Scenes from a Receding Past.
KEIZO HINO, *Isle of Dreams.*
KAZUSHI HOSAKA, *Plainsong.*
ALDOUS HUXLEY, *Antic Hay.*
    Crome Yellow.
    Point Counter Point.
    Those Barren Leaves.
    Time Must Have a Stop.
NAOYUKI II, *The Shadow of a Blue Cat.*
GERT JONKE, *The Distant Sound.*
    Geometric Regional Novel.
    Homage to Czerny.
    The System of Vienna.
JACQUES JOUET, *Mountain R.*
    Savage.
    Upstaged.

MIEKO KANAI, *The Word Book.*
YORAM KANIUK, *Life on Sandpaper.*
HUGH KENNER, *Flaubert.*
    Joyce and Beckett: The Stoic Comedians.
    Joyce's Voices.
DANILO KIŠ, *The Attic.*
    Garden, Ashes.
    The Lute and the Scars
    Psalm 44.
    A Tomb for Boris Davidovich.
ANITA KONKKA, *A Fool's Paradise.*
GEORGE KONRÁD, *The City Builder.*
TADEUSZ KONWICKI, *A Minor Apocalypse.*
    The Polish Complex.
MENIS KOUMANDAREAS, *Koula.*
ELAINE KRAF, *The Princess of 72nd Street.*
JIM KRUSOE, *Iceland.*
AYŞE KULIN, *Farewell: A Mansion in*
    Occupied Istanbul.
EMILIO LASCANO TEGUI, *On Elegance*
    While Sleeping.
ERIC LAURRENT, *Do Not Touch.*
VIOLETTE LEDUC, *La Bâtarde.*
EDOUARD LEVÉ, *Autoportrait.*
    Suicide.
MARIO LEVI, *Istanbul Was a Fairy Tale.*
DEBORAH LEVY, *Billy and Girl.*
JOSÉ LEZAMA LIMA, *Paradiso.*
ROSA LIKSOM, *Dark Paradise.*
OSMAN LINS, *Avalovara.*
    The Queen of the Prisons of Greece.
ALF MAC LOCHLAINN,
    The Corpus in the Library.
    Out of Focus.
RON LOEWINSOHN, *Magnetic Field(s).*
MINA LOY, *Stories and Essays of Mina Loy.*
D. KEITH MANO, *Take Five.*
MICHELINE AHARONIAN MARCOM,
    The Mirror in the Well.
BEN MARCUS,
    The Age of Wire and String.
WALLACE MARKFIELD,
    Teitlebaum's Window.
    To an Early Grave.
DAVID MARKSON, *Reader's Block.*
    Wittgenstein's Mistress.
CAROLE MASO, *AVA.*
LADISLAV MATEJKA AND KRYSTYNA
    POMORSKA, EDS.,
    Readings in Russian Poetics:
        Formalist and Structuralist Views.
HARRY MATHEWS, *Cigarettes.*
    The Conversions.
    The Human Country: New and
        Collected Stories.
    The Journalist.
    My Life in CIA.
    Singular Pleasures.
    The Sinking of the Odradek
        Stadium.
    Tlooth.

JOSEPH MCELROY, *Night Soul and Other Stories.*

ABDELWAHAB MEDDEB, *Talismano.*

GERHARD MEIER, *Isle of the Dead.*

HERMAN MELVILLE, *The Confidence-Man.*

AMANDA MICHALOPOULOU, *I'd Like.*

STEVEN MILLHAUSER, *The Barnum Museum.*
In the Penny Arcade.

RALPH J. MILLS, JR., *Essays on Poetry.*

MOMUS, *The Book of Jokes.*

CHRISTINE MONTALBETTI, *The Origin of Man.*
Western.

OLIVE MOORE, *Spleen.*

NICHOLAS MOSLEY, *Accident.*
Assassins.
Catastrophe Practice.
Experience and Religion.
A Garden of Trees.
Hopeful Monsters.
Imago Bird.
Impossible Object.
Inventing God.
Judith.
Look at the Dark.
Natalie Natalia.
Serpent.
Time at War.

WARREN MOTTE,
Fables of the Novel: French Fiction since 1990.
Fiction Now: The French Novel in the 21st Century.
Oulipo: A Primer of Potential Literature.

GERALD MURNANE, *Barley Patch.*
Inland.

YVES NAVARRE, *Our Share of Time.*
Sweet Tooth.

DOROTHY NELSON, *In Night's City.*
Tar and Feathers.

ESHKOL NEVO, *Homesick.*

WILFRIDO D. NOLLEDO, *But for the Lovers.*

FLANN O'BRIEN, *At Swim-Two-Birds.*
The Best of Myles.
The Dalkey Archive.
The Hard Life.
The Poor Mouth.
The Third Policeman.

CLAUDE OLLIER, *The Mise-en-Scène.*
Wert and the Life Without End.

GIOVANNI ORELLI, *Walaschek's Dream.*

PATRIK OUŘEDNÍK, *Europeana.*
The Opportune Moment, 1855.

BORIS PAHOR, *Necropolis.*

FERNANDO DEL PASO, *News from the Empire.*
Palinuro of Mexico.

ROBERT PINGET, *The Inquisitory.*
Mahu or The Material.
Trio.

MANUEL PUIG, *Betrayed by Rita Hayworth.*

The Buenos Aires Affair.
Heartbreak Tango.

RAYMOND QUENEAU, *The Last Days.*
Odile.
Pierrot Mon Ami.
Saint Glinglin.

ANN QUIN, *Berg.*
Passages.
Three.
Tripticks.

ISHMAEL REED, *The Free-Lance Pallbearers.*
The Last Days of Louisiana Red.
Ishmael Reed: The Plays.
Juice!
Reckless Eyeballing.
The Terrible Threes.
The Terrible Twos.
Yellow Back Radio Broke-Down.

JASIA REICHARDT, *15 Journeys Warsaw to London.*

NOËLLE REVAZ, *With the Animals.*

JOÃO UBALDO RIBEIRO, *House of the Fortunate Buddhas.*

JEAN RICARDOU, *Place Names.*

RAINER MARIA RILKE, *The Notebooks of Malte Laurids Brigge.*

JULIÁN RÍOS, *The House of Ulysses.*
Larva: A Midsummer Night's Babel.
Poundemonium.
Procession of Shadows.

AUGUSTO ROA BASTOS, *I the Supreme.*

DANIËL ROBBERECHTS, *Arriving in Avignon.*

JEAN ROLIN, *The Explosion of the Radiator Hose.*

OLIVIER ROLIN, *Hotel Crystal.*

ALIX CLEO ROUBAUD, *Alix's Journal.*

JACQUES ROUBAUD, *The Form of a City Changes Faster, Alas, Than the Human Heart.*
The Great Fire of London.
Hortense in Exile.
Hortense Is Abducted.
The Loop.
Mathematics:
The Plurality of Worlds of Lewis.
The Princess Hoppy.
Some Thing Black.

RAYMOND ROUSSEL, *Impressions of Africa.*

VEDRANA RUDAN, *Night.*

STIG SÆTERBAKKEN, *Siamese.*
Self Control.

LYDIE SALVAYRE, *The Company of Ghosts.*
The Lecture.
The Power of Flies.

LUIS RAFAEL SÁNCHEZ, *Macho Camacho's Beat.*

SEVERO SARDUY, *Cobra & Maitreya.*

NATHALIE SARRAUTE,
Do You Hear Them?
Martereau.
The Planetarium.

SELECTED DALKEY ARCHIVE TITLES

FOR A FULL LIST OF PUBLICATIONS, VISIT:
www.dalkeyarchive.com